Praise for Melissa Schroeder's
Grace Under Pressure

5 Nymphs "Grace Under Pressure is sexy and fun, filled with everything a reader expects in a great romantic story. Tension and passion abound when these well defined characters are brought together. Ms. Schroeder has penned a fabulous tale that will have you laughing from the very first sentence. " ~ *Water Nymph, Literary Nymphs*

"Melissa Schroeder is a genius ... I found myself laughing out loud and blushing all at the same time. For a great romantic comedy, Grace Under Pressure really delivers!" ~ *Talia Ricci, Joyfully Reviewed*

4 Ribbons "Melissa Schroeder has crafted a tale that is a remarkable blend of thrilling suspenseful action, humorous comical relief and delicious sexual encounters that will curl your toes." ~ Contessa, Romance Junkies,

4 Cups "This is one riveting tale that keeps you clinging to your seat all the way thru it." ~ *Lainey, Coffee Time Reviews*

4 Angels *"Grace Under Pressure* by Melissa Schroeder is at its best with so much sexual attraction yet it has suspense in it that will surprise every reader." ~ *Lena C, Fallen Angel Reviews*

"Hilariously funny and so hot it sizzles. You can't beat that combination." ~ *Karen Kelley, Close Encounters of the Sexy Kind, Brava*

Grace Under Pressure

Melissa Schroeder

A SAMHAIN PUBLISHING, LTD. publication.

Samhain Publishing, Ltd.
512 Forest Lake Drive
Warner Robins, GA 31093
www.samhainpublishing.com

Grace Under Pressure
Copyright © 2006 by Melissa Schroeder
Print ISBN: 1-59998-361-3
Digital ISBN: 1-59998-239-0

Editing by Sara Reinke
Cover by Scott Carpenter

First Samhain Publishing, Ltd. electronic publication: November 2006
First Samhain Publishing, Ltd. print publication: February 2007

Dedication

To the Lakehouse Girls: Darese Cotton, Mary Beth Lee, Karen Kelley, Sheila Curlin and Shelley Bradley. Your enthusiasm, support, and love, not to mention the homemade pizza and wine, make it so much easier to brave the publishing world.

Chapter One

"And what did you say to your class after you substituted the word *erection* for *election?*" Grace's best friend, Julia, asked during their lunchtime phone conversation.

When she'd awoken thirty minutes late that morning, the sun burning holes through her eyelids because she'd forgotten to close the blinds, Grace had known it wasn't going to be a good day. When she sprayed the hairspray under her arm, then deodorant on her hair, she figured things couldn't get much worse.

"First of all, I did *not* substitute the word," she said. "You make it sound as if I did it on purpose. It's not my goal in life to embarrass myself in front of a classroom full of college freshmen." A classroom of freshman that happened to include Chad Albert, the college president's son. The muffled sounds she heard over the phone made her suspicious. "Stop laughing! It's not funny."

"I'm sorry, Grace. I really didn't mean to laugh, but you have to admit it's funny."

"I will do no such thing." She winced at the prim sound of her voice.

She had noticed that spinsterish tone creeping in more often over the last couple years. If she wasn't careful, she was going to end up adopting twenty cats and yelling at kids who stepped on her lawn. "It was just so humiliating. Thank the Lord it was close enough to the end of class that I could just dismiss them. Unfortunately, I have to give the same lecture to my five-thirty class."

"Just block out the memory," Julia suggested. "You know, like you did when you had that unfortunate incident at graduation."

Grace lowered her head and pounded it on the desk. There were a lot of things that she loved about living and working in the same small college town in which she spent most of her life—the familiar faces, the regular routine, and the security. The fact that almost everyone she knew had attended her high school graduation and witnessed her valedictorian walk-up to the stage, with her dress and gown stuffed in her pantyhose, was not one of them.

She just wished she had worn underwear that day.

"I'd have no problem forgetting about graduation, if everyone else would let me," she muttered through clenched teeth. "Why do you bring it up every time I do something like this?"

"Ah, come on, Grace. I was just kidding. Why don't I make it up to you? Dinner, my treat."

"I can't. I told you I have a five-thirty lecture."

"Yeah, the erection lecture."

"Shut up."

"I'm just joking."

"Well," Grace said. "I need to get going. I have to go over to Mom and Dad's house and give the keys to their new tenant."

"Okay, but I owe you dinner. How about tomorrow?"

"Sounds good." She looked at her date book and groaned when she saw her Friday night schedule. "Oh, no, I can't do that. Dr. Peterson is having some dinner thing at his house tomorrow night. How about Saturday?"

"That's a deal. But, you could always blow off Pesky Peterson and come over here."

"Nope. Peterson has some big announcement tomorrow night. Gotta be there for that."

₨₩

With the Beatles blaring on her speakers, Grace drove to her parents' house, which was located about ten minutes from the college and across the street from her own house. She drew in a deep breath, enjoying the crisp fall scents that drifted through her open window.

She parked her 1968 restored convertible Bug in the driveway in front of her parents' house. Pristine and neat, it was like all the little homes in the neighborhood, though each possessed its own identity. She loved everything about it, from the familiar creaks in the floor to the wraparound porch.

A hedge of bushes lined the passenger side of the driveway, but the opposite, identical row had been destroyed by one too many renters trampling on them. A warm wind whipped around her face. She cursed when it tugged at her curls, no doubt pulling a few from the bun into which she had struggled to imprison them. Knowing it would do no good to fight them, she gave a mental shrug and walked up the path to the front porch.

It was two-story farm house, with white aluminum siding which replaced the once wooden slats she and her brother, Gabriel used to curse each time they'd had to help paint them. The no-nonsense black trim contrasted with the brightness of the white siding. A massive wraparound porch that had once been filled with potted ferns and impatiens, a couple of rocking

9

chairs and a swing, was now bare except for a few dried leaves and one coffee cup.

Four cement steps led up to the porch, elevating it and allowing for a flowerbed with a hedge of Texas sage lining either side.

She eyed the cup again and judged the distance. It sat on the edge and would be just as easy to grab it from where she stood as to go up on the porch. Bracing herself on the bottom edge of the porch, she leaned over the soft blue-green leaves of the Texas sage to grab it, balancing on one foot. She had the damn thing within her reach when her left foot slipped. Losing her grip, she tumbled head first into the bushes. Hands out in front of her, she landed on the hard ground, her palms taking the brunt of the fall. Several branches lashed her face, and a small rock bit into one of her hands. She lifted them, inspecting them for scrapes and cuts while balancing on her elbows, her rear end slightly elevated because her knees had landed on the pavement. She wiped away the dirt, finding no serious cuts.

She hoped no one witnessed her lying with her backside sticking up in the air. Knowing her luck though, the Board of Regents from the university was probably lined up behind her.

"I always heard that Texas was a friendly state," said an amused male voice. "I just didn't realize how friendly."

୨୦ଓ

Ren Morello watched Grace push herself out of the tangle of bushes, try to straighten her ugly, brown, shapeless suit and turn to face him. At least, he assumed this was his new landlady. It was a real shame she was wearing that suit. The stiff tweed material resembled the color of mud, which did nothing for the woman.

Once she stood, the material fell away from her curves giving her an almost boxy appearance. From the view he had walking up the path, he was pretty sure there was a nice rounded ass beneath it.

Her skirt was twisted and hiked up a few inches, revealing a lacy slip and a hole in her hose. He watched her try to pull her unruly red hair back into the neat little bun on her head. A sprinkling of freckles ran across her nose, along with a few scratches from some of the branches. When she finally looked him in the eye, he noticed that, unlike her mother, who had sky-blue eyes, Grace possessed eyes the color of whiskey, lightened by golden flecks. They turned up slightly at the corners, giving him the impression of something definitely feline.

"I take it that you are Ren Morello," she said in a slightly husky voice that vibrated down his spine, "What am I saying? Of course you are. That would be about par for the day." She raised her hands again, a nervous gesture, trying to pull her dark red curls under control.

"Ren Morello," he said, offering his hand to shake.

"Grace Michaels." She stepped forward and firmly shook his hand.

She plastered on a professional smile that did nothing to diminish the fullness of her lips. They were as lush as the rest of her body. Only a smudge of lipstick on the upper lip marked them—the rest looked as if she had eaten it off, worrying. "I assure you I am a lot more professional than I appear at the moment."

"Oh," he said, his lips curving slightly. "You look professional enough to me."

Her face reddened, those lips flattening into a straight line and he thought he heard her mutter. "A professional what?"

11

"I assume you want a walk-through?" she asked.

He followed her up the stairs onto the wraparound porch, watching the natural sway of her hips as she climbed the steps. Damn, but she was sexy. Grace Michaels had a figure that reminded him of Marilyn Monroe or Rosalind Russell.

Although the suit was almost asexual in its design, he had a fantastic view of that ass with the rough brown material stretched tight across it. He had also seen one shapely leg when her skirt had hiked up. He glanced down at those legs, covered by her skirt, thinking it had been a long time since he'd slipped his hand up a skirt to caress the soft skin behind a woman's knee. He shook his head to clear it, wondering what the hell he was thinking.

She wasn't his usual sort of woman. He tended to date women who were lean and hard. Athleticism had been a turn-on to him from his first time in the backseat of his car with Janet Rice, the star of the girls' high school track team. Women he dated were tall, but a little on the thin side, with no more than a handful or mouthful, however you looked at the situation. The most important thing about them was they understood it was casual. A serious relationship was something he did not want and had not wanted since his divorce.

Besides, first impressions never failed with him before and Grace Michaels reeked of commitment. She possessed the aura of a suburbanite. She reminded him of chocolate chip cookies and PTA meetings, the type who would settle down, have two-point-five kids and a two-car garage.

He could tell by looking at Grace, her conservative suit and that serious expression, she didn't fool around. But, then again, there was nothing wrong with appreciating the view.

The clank of keys hitting the porch floor brought his attention back to Grace as she bent over to retrieve them. He zeroed back to her backside once more. The fabric stretched tighter this time and he definitely detected a fully rounded heart shape.

A vision of holding those rounded cheeks in his hands, those shapely legs wrapped around his waist as he braced her against a wall, and pumped into her, streaked across his mind before he could prevent it.

She straightened herself and turned around to say something to him, but whatever it was died on her lips when she realized where he had been staring. Ren slowly slid his gaze up her body to meet her eyes, and noticed once again that her face was fire engine red. She abruptly turned, unlocked the door and walked into the house. He took a deep breath, trying to steady his usually controllable libido and followed her through the door, shutting it with an almost silent click.

ℛℭ

Grace's face still burned as she showed Ren through her parents' house. Never in all her years had she been so embarrassed. And, considering her history, that was saying a lot. As he inspected the kitchen, she remembered the look on his face when she turned around and found him staring at her rear end. She thought she might have detected a hint of appreciation.

Surely not. Lean, hungry, virile men were never interested in her. They liked supermodel wannabes, like the ones her brother dated. Perfect bodies with little minds were Gabriel's type.

That was okay. She wasn't really interested in Ren Morello anyway. Okay, so he was attractive. Very attractive. Didn't mean that she had to be interested in him. She had a career to worry about. She didn't have time to pay attention to the exquisite hunk of man walking around her mother's kitchen.

And he *was* exquisite. He had short black hair, graying a little at the temples, and chocolate brown eyes with crinkles at the corners that could be from either smiling or glaring. She would bet on the latter.

His slightly crooked nose looked like it had been broken more than once, and he had full, sensuous lips. If he hadn't been so masculine in all his other features, she was sure that you could term those lips as almost feminine. He was tall, at least six feet, most of which was legs. She'd never lusted after a man's legs, usually focusing on a man's mind first, but she truly wanted to see what they looked like out of the body-hugging denim. Worn and soft, it stretched tightly across his butt, rode low on his hips, and cupped his sex in the most disturbing manner.

Her pulse accelerated a few beats per minute and she took a deep breath to try to steady it. Good Lord! Why the hell was she thinking about how nicely his jeans outlined that particular part of his body? She needed to stay calm and cool. Being attracted to the stud renting her parents' house wasn't a smart thing to do.

It was just her luck that the first attractive man she met in several months had been spending his first introduction to her staring at what she considered her worst body feature. Of course, she wasn't interested, she reassured herself—again. So what if he had a body of a god and milk chocolate eyes? She didn't care. Just because her blood warmed at the thought of running her hands down his muscled back to cup his ass—and it was a wonderful ass—didn't mean she wanted to jump his bones.

She shook herself out of her musings. She did not care about Ren Morello and his exquisite ass.

Really, she didn't.

He inspected the oven like he actually was going to use it for something other than reheating pizza. Single, good-looking men in this town didn't have to cook for themselves. Available men you had not dated, and to whom you were not related, were a scarcity in a small town like Cannon, Texas. One this attractive, and with a job like Chief of Police, would be a single girl's dream come true.

Well, single girls who cared about that sort of thing, she told herself. Which did not include her. She cared most about her career, she thought, straightening her shoulders and tilting her chin.

It would be best if she kept that in mind. The sooner she was out of there and back to work the better.

ഇറ

Ten minutes later, they'd finished looking at the master bedroom upstairs. "Two of the other rooms are relatively the same size," she said. "But this one is smaller because my parents redid the bathroom. There's another full bath at the end of the hall. The only room that gets a lot of sun is the front bedroom. I know, because it was mine. I took the sun because it was the only other one not next to my parents' room. But the oak tree out front helps most of the year."

"And it must have been pretty easy to sneak out using that oak," he said, noticing her mischievous smile. "But I'm sure you would never think of something like that."

She raised an eyebrow. "I sprained my ankle sneaking back in one night."

15

"Oh? How did you do that?"

"Well," she said, motioning for him to take the lead down the stairs. "Julia, my best friend, thought it would be cool to skinny-dip in the high school pool."

He reached the bottom step, and turned to face her as she stopped about five steps from the bottom. "I'm amazed you would do something like that," he said.

"You mean, sneak out of the house?" she asked.

He didn't respond right away. "No." The corners of his mouth curved slightly. "Skinny-dipping. You look more like a girl who would be in bed by nine at night." He perused her, from her head slowly down her body. "And, I mean in bed and asleep. Red, you look like the type of woman most likely to report someone skinny-dipping."

She pursed her lips. "Don't call me Red."

"Let's get back to the skinny-dipping part," he said, pushing her just a little further.

"Oh." Her face flamed once again. "Well, Julia forgot to tell me to get the key, so we couldn't get in. You know, Dad was the athletic director, so he had all the keys to the department."

"Oh," he said. "But you said you sprained your ankle."

"Yes, I was climbing up the oak out front when Julia said something to me. I turned to face her and lost my balance. I landed on the roof of the porch, which woke up the dogs and Dad. Turned out that she was trying to tell me to be careful."

He laughed.

"Well," she said, prissiness creeping back in her voice. "At least now I'm not that clumsy anymore."

She picked an imaginary piece of lint off her suit, studied it intently and then flicked it away.

"Yeah," he said. "What happened out front earlier, Red?"

Ren wasn't even trying to hide that he was laughing at her. Her spine stiffened and fire snapped in her eyes. "That was just an accident," she said in a schoolmarm tone that reminded him of his fourth grade teacher. With Grace, that prissy tone in her husky voice caused his dick to stand at attention. It also made him want to tease her more. He just couldn't help himself. "And I told you not to call me Red."

She put her hand on the banister and took a step. The heel of her right shoe somehow caught the edge of the step. She catapulted forward, her eyes lit with surprise and her arms wind-milling.

He held his hands out and caught her by the waist, trying to stop the inevitable. But he lost his footing and suddenly flew backward, landing on the hard wooden floor. The air rushed out of his lungs, leaving him gasping for air.

Before he could catch his breath, Grace landed on him with a thud, smacking his nose with her forehead. He blinked, shook his head once or twice, trying to focus his eyes. looking as dazed as Grace felt as she leaned up on her elbows.

He suddenly realized he was right about all the curves under that ugly suit and they were, at the moment, pressing up against him. She was round and warm, and it felt entirely too comfortable having her on top of him. Ren knew he should ignore those curves and the soft warm woman on top of him, but he just didn't have the willpower.

Despite the ringing in his ears, and the stars circling in front of his eyes, he laughed. I have to say again, Red," he said, smacking an outraged Grace on her rear end. "I'm really amazed how friendly Texas actually is."

ℰ⃝ℛ

Grace shut the door to her office and sighed, releasing all the tension and frustration from the day. She dumped her briefcase and sat behind her desk. It was now close to eight at night, and her day had started before eight that morning. Kicking off her pumps, she leaned back in her chair and rubbed her temples.

If she'd planned on humiliating herself when she woke this morning, she was sure it would be considered a banner day. There was no possible way things could get worse. As she closed her eyes and started mentally preparing for tomorrow and her lectures, a knock sounded at her door.

"Come in," she yelled, knowing anyone in the small building that housed the history department would have to have a key.

The door opened, and Darian Daniel Dawson, her ex-fiancé, stood in the doorway.

Okay, she was wrong. Her day could get worse.

Chapter Two

"Working late, Grace?" Darian asked.

She'd only seen him briefly at conferences in the past few years, but nothing had changed. He was wearing one of his Brooks Brothers suits, tailored to perfection without one wrinkle or crease. Spending all day driving in the car wouldn't cause Darian Daniel Dawson to have something so plebeian as a wrinkled suit.

The tailored suit fit well over his tennis-pro body. He was lean and athletic, but lacked the presence of strength. She didn't know if she made that observation based on his character, physique, or a combination of both. Even though the west Texas winds had been blowing hard that day, his blond hair had not a strand out of place. The snake-oil salesman smile didn't reach his eyes, which had the same cold and calculated look he had given her when he'd told her his cheating was her fault. His tie, suit and shirt coordinated well, as usual, and brought out the blueness of those eyes.

"Always. What the hell are you doing here?" she asked without any heat.

"Gracie, Gracie. Are you still hostile after eight years?" he said, closing the door and walking toward her.

She hated when he used that nickname. He'd once told her it was uncouth to change a name as classy as *Grace* to *Gracie*. He used it to let her know he thought himself superior to her.

What the hell had she been thinking when she was with him all those years ago? Oh, yeah, she'd been young, stupid, and thought she was in love. Darian, or the Triple D as Julia called him, had apparently thought their relationship would be like his parents' marriage and had gotten a head start with Grace's research assistant right on her own desk, blaming her lack of response to him in bed as the reason for his cheating.

"Listen, Darian, I'm really tired and I've had a long day. I just wondered why you decided to drive all the way up to Cannon, a place you called the cultural armpit of America."

"I'm doing some research in the area."

"You, research?" Grace asked, snorting again.

"Really. I just thought I would come by and give you a heads up."

"Heads up?" she said, and then all the barrels locked into place and her eyes narrowed. "You're Peterson's big announcement tomorrow. What are you going to do, talk at one of the lecture series?"

"Yes. But I took a sabbatical from UT this year. I decided to relocate up here to do a little research. Peterson thought it would be great if I taught a class or two." Before she could say anything, Darian turned and walked toward the door. "I just thought I should let you know. I didn't want you to embarrass yourself tomorrow night."

Then, he was gone.

"Well, hell," she said to her empty office.

෨෬

A day after his encounter with Grace, Ren's nose still throbbed and his back ached as he drove to the office. He officially didn't start working until Monday, but thought he should show up and get his bearings.

Cannon was a typical, small Texas town. Each street pretty much resembled the next. Most homes in a place like Cannon were modest in size and well kept. For what little towns lacked in wealth, they made up in pride. Yards were trimmed and several had wooden football signs with numbers representing the player who lived in the house. He knew tonight more trucks than cars would be parked out front of each one of these houses.

Cannon reminded him of several little Texas towns˘ he'd been through. As he turned on Main Street, he found the police department on his right, and across the street from the Dairy Queen.

Someone had parked in his designated spot, so he slid into the Deputy on Duty slot, assuming that was who parked in his.

After getting out of his truck, Ren studied the weathered Cannon Police Department building. Tex was right. The mayor had told Ren the place needed a facelift, but Ren thought it might need a whole body lift. Two layers of paint were peeling and there were more shingles missing than actually on the roof. The painted window to the office was faded with time and even if he squinted, he was not sure he could make out the name. Businesses that lined each side of the office appeared to have been remodeled within the last few years, making the deterioration of his building even more obvious.

He walked through the front door and found a rather large woman sitting behind a metal, battle-scarred desk. Her hair was dyed pink and she had it styled in a beehive. She wore black cat glasses, outlined with rhinestones.

Her makeup was a splash of colors with no clear purpose, though the orange eye shadow seemed to be tie in with the ugly green-and-orange flowered shirt she was wearing. Bright pink pumps peeked out from beneath the desk.

"Can I help you?" she asked through very red lips.

"You've got to be Ms. Janey," he said, stepping forward with an outstretched hand. "I'm Ren Morello."

She stared at his hand and then her eyes traveled back to his face. Her gaze made him nervous. After a minute or two, he felt like fool holding out his hand, so he dropped it.

"Ren Morello? The new Chief of Police? You can't be him," she said, dismissing him and turning toward her monitor. "He's not supposed to be here until Monday."

"I just so happened to make it a few days early because my movers are going to be here on Saturday. I thought I would get a jump start."

She turned around to face him with a skeptical look on her face. "Yeah, I'm sure you want to get the little wife settled in the old Michaels house."

"You know I'm divorced. Tex told me you would know everything that was in my file and if I didn't want the whole town to know certain details to leave them out."

Tex had also told him Ms. Janey was somewhat of a paranoid. He had told Ren she had spent years trying to prove who killed JFK. She was also convinced that aliens had once landed about ten miles outside of town.

The skepticism faded and her face softened. She stood and offered him a hand.

"I'm Ms Janey, but you already knew that," she said as she shook his hand. Jeez, she had the grip of a linebacker. "Welcome to Cannon. I'm glad you're finally here. I've had your office closed up or Deputy Jenkins would screw everything up in there."

She tugged at a chain around her neck and pulled out what must have been a forty inch chain holding dozens of keys. Where on earth she had hidden them he had no idea, and he really didn't want to know.

"He thought he was in charge when Chief Banister left. Thought it was no longer proper for me to call him by his Christian name. I told that boy I'd changed his diapers and wiped his bottom when I worked in the Cannon First Baptist Church nursery, but he didn't seemed to think that mattered." She unlocked the door and stood aside to let him in.

It was as small as he expected. Cannon only had forty-five thousand people in town and that was counting the college kids, so he'd not expected anything great. But what he found looked like Bambi's nightmare. The walls were covered with dark wooden paneling, which must have been installed twenty years ago. The smell of stale cigarettes permeated the area and his desk was a replica of the desk Ms. Janey had, except his was an olive green and dented in the front.

On the far wall, a corkboard held pictures of wanted felons. That, too, looked like it had been there a couple of decades, judging by the pictures. The filing cabinet was a green metal, and two of the four drawers were hanging open. Files were stacked on top, filled with yellowed papers, and he shuddered to think of the work that needed to be done.

But the crowning jewel was a moth-eaten deer head left by his predecessor. One of the antlers was hanging upside down and the left eye was missing. It looked like it was going to fall off of the nail from which it hung.

"Sort of takes your breath away, doesn't it?" Ms. Janey asked. He could hear the amusement in her voice. "Old Chief Banister got a little lazy during the last few years."

"The last few?" Ren asked quirking an eyebrow, and Ms. Janey cackled. "It looks like he took off the last two decades."

"Yeah, well, the man is seventy-five as of last April. I was so happy when little Tex got us more money for a new chief. We couldn't get anyone to fill the job for the money and Jed just didn't feel like he could leave us in a lurch without a chief. But then, he had the heart attack and the doc said no more work."

"What about one of the deputies?" he asked, starting to worry about the men and women working for him. Tex had called them young and inexperienced, but eager to learn. He hoped they had some kind of training.

"Oh, I don't think little Tex could get re-elected mayor if he made one of them chief," she said and he wondered how she could call a man who was at least six foot four and weighed well over three-hundred pounds *little*. "Don't get me wrong, they're good boys. But they're boys...well, except for Janice and Carrie. As I was saying, we needed a man for the job. Which," she said, perusing him from his feet to his head, "from the looks of it, little Tex got us. You're going to be in high demand around this town when the word gets out. I'd have a go at you myself if I was twenty years younger."

"Ah, Ms. Janey," he said, smiling. "I'm afraid you are too much woman for me. I don't think I could keep up with you."

She threw her head back and let out another loud cackle. "Don't you worry about it. Mr. Beau has been taking care of me for close to forty years. Don't know another man who could keep up."

Before he could reply, the front door slammed opened then shut.

"Ms. Janey!" yelled a slightly whiney male voice. "Who the hell is parked in my space? It better not be some damn college jackass."

Ren followed Ms. Janey out into the front office. A scrawny man who was no more than five-seven, and dressed in a tan deputy's uniform stood at the other desk in the office. The tan hat he wore rode low over his prominent ears, looking as if he had taken his daddy's hat by mistake. Aviator glasses sat on a very thin nose. He was looking through the drawers, slamming each shut when he didn't find what he needed.

"Where are the fucking parking tickets?" he asked without looking up.

"I really don't think you should be talking like that around Ms. Janey," Ren said.

The deputy looked up when he heard Ren's voice. He whipped off his glasses, threw them on the desk and settled his hands on his skinny hips. His eyes moved from Ren to Ms. Janey. Clear gray eyes narrowed as he looked back at Ren.

"Just who the hell are you and why was Ms. Janey letting you in the chief's office? That idiot won't be here until Monday."

Ms. Janey sighed as Ren stepped forward.

"Well, it isn't every day I am insulted twice in less than two minutes. I'm Ren Morello, the jackass who's parked in your space and the idiot you're working for."

He fought the urge to smile as he watched the deputy's Adam's apple bob up and down as he swallowed nervously. His gray eyes shifted from side to side as if trying to find an escape. Had he ever been that young?

"Man, I can't believe I just did that. I am *so* sorry," the deputy said while pulling his hat off, revealing a head of curly blond hair. He nervously shifted the hat from hand to hand.

"I think we can let it pass," Ren said.

"Barney here always did have a problem with his mouth," Ms. Janey said from behind Ren.

"Ms. Janey, I told you to call me Deputy Jenkins," he said through clenched teeth.

"Are you telling me I have a deputy by the name of Barney?" Ren asked.

Deputy Barney nodded, his blond curls bobbing up and down. Ren had wanted small town roots with colorful characters. Sometimes you got what you wanted in spades.

₮℞

Julia Jacobs sat in her comfy leather chair in her home office, sipping coffee while she enjoyed the quiet of her morning. With her work, she was used to late nights and early mornings. She was reviewing some revisions for her latest book when the phone rang.

"You are never going to guess who is in town and what Pesky Peterson's big surprise is," Grace said, without saying hello.

"Who and what are you talking about?" It must have been something upsetting because Grace never used Julia's nickname for the head of the department out loud.

"The Triple D made a visit to my office last night. He seems to think it'd be a great idea to teach for a semester at the college and do research in the area."

"What the hell is he researching and what was Peterson thinking?"

"Well, I can't blame Peterson. He doesn't know the whole story. I think all he sees is Darian Daniel Dawson, super PhD."

"What does he do, leap stacks of periodicals in a single bound?" Julia said dryly.

Grace snorted, and Julia relaxed. She knew she was the only one who knew all the circumstances involving their breakup. Though Grace was very close to her mother, she had only confided in Julia about what had happened. Only Julia had known exactly how devastated Grace was when she returned to Cannon.

"So, what are you going to do about the dinner tonight? You could blow it off on principle and drink tequila with me."

"No, that would give Darian too much satisfaction," Grace said. "I don't care he's here, I just don't trust him."

"For good reason."

"But you could come to the dinner with me tonight."

"Not unless I was heavily medicated," Julia replied, dryly.

"Oh, come on, I need support."

"You do not. You are the true Super PhD."

"Yeah, well, I am not sure about the leaping of periodicals, but I can fly down stairs."

"Now what are you talking about?" Julia asked.

"Well, I met the new Chief of Police yesterday."

"Oh, yeah, how did that go, by the way?"

"Well, let's just say the most eligible, exquisitely formed bachelor was subjected to a view of my worst asset, no pun intended."

"I'm sure it's not as bad as you think it was," Julia said, trying to reassure her friend.

"Well, the first view he had of me was my ass sticking up in the air. Then, I tripped and fell down the stairs, landing on top of him." Grace let out an aggravated sigh. "It was *not* my finest hour."

"Did he get mad?"

"No, apparently he thought it was hilarious and said something both times about Texas being a friendly state. It doesn't really matter, because he's not my type."

"What do you mean? What type is he?" Julia asked.

"Well, he's over six feet tall, dark hair, chocolate brown eyes with the body of Adonis. Like I said, not my type and I'm sure I'm not his."

"Why not? Grace, I think you don't understand anything about men."

"Oh, yeah, and you do?"

"Okay, so I don't have much field experience, but I have studied them for work." Julia knew she was sounding defensive but she didn't care.

"Oh, crap. I'm late for my Western Civ lecture. I have to get going. Talk to you later."

Julia hung up her phone and thought about the situation. She wasn't so sure Grace would stick to her guns when it came to avoiding that weasel, Darian. She made a mental note to call Grace's brother Gabriel for backup.

ℴ⇣

By the end of the day, Grace was cranky from spending most of it sweating like a hog. A warm front had blown through west Texas, causing the temperatures to rise to close to eighty degrees. It was a policy of the college not to turn on the air conditioning unless the temperature went over eighty, so most of the classrooms were unbearable. Especially since the windows didn't open in the small history building where she taught.

She rushed home and changed into a loose-fitting, yellow cotton dress, which was far more comfortable than the suits she wore to teach. Also, she could wear sandals and no pantyhose. She preferred stockings or thigh-highs, but she'd gone through every one of them this morning, and couldn't find one without a run or hole in them. By the end of the day, her pantyhose had twisted uncomfortably and she vowed to get online to order some more, since the closest mall was a forty-five minute drive.

Then, she literally let her hair down, pulling out the pins and rubbing her scalp. It was really quite scary. The humidity had caused her already big, curly hair to expand to enormous proportions. To keep from looking like an over-the-hill rodeo queen, she pulled the unruly red mass behind her and tied it loosely with a ribbon.

Sometimes she thought about cutting it off. Then, Julia would remind her that she'd done that once and looked like a red Q-tip. She grabbed a bottle of lip-gloss, and smeared some on her lips, deciding that was the best it was going to get.

After squirting some perfume on, hoping that would mask her body odor, she let Sam, her dog, back into the house.

She made sure he had enough water, and tried to ignore the rude look he sent her for leaving him alone for the second night in a row.

"I'll be back by eight, I promise. Go on back to your room and take a nap." Grace's old bed from her childhood, equipped with silky sheets, had been taken over by Sam.

She grabbed her purse and keys. She opened the door and almost ran into Ren with his fist in the air about to knock.

"If I would have known you were waiting by the door, I would have been over earlier, Red," he said.

Chapter Three

Grace turned to lock the door and Ren allowed his gaze to travel down, appreciating the view she afforded him. She stood so close to him, the heat from her body seeped through the thin fabric of her dress and against him, and he could smell the sweet fragrance of her perfume in a heady cloud around her. *Why the hell did I come here?* he thought, annoyed with himself. They weren't face-to-face even five seconds, and already he was undressing her in his mind.

She turned, stepped around Ren, and started walking briskly. "I'm having dinner over at Dr. Peterson's house and I'm late."

The fantasy in which he slipped his hands up beneath her flirty skirt, letting his palms follow the generous contours of her thighs up towards her hips immediately dissolved. "Peterson?" he asked, and why did he suddenly feel disappointed? "Is that who you're dating?"

Grace abruptly stopped, causing Ren to run into her back. She turned looked at him and started to laugh. It was a rich throaty laugh, not the little giggle he was used to hearing from the women he dated. It was the type of laugh men loved to hear in the bedroom. Full-bodied and low enough to remind him of just how much he liked to tease in bed.

"Um," she said, trying to stop laughing. "No. He's the head of the department. He has a huge announcement to tell us and we're to be subjected to his wife's cooking. And I missed lunch today, so I might even eat some of her food."

"Well, if you're hungry, her cooking shouldn't matter."

She grimaced. "Yeah right," she said. "If she ever offers you any of her canned pickles, don't eat them. Dr. Gump had his stomached pumped last fall."

Grace turned and started back down the path to the sidewalk, the skirt of her filmy dress flapping behind her. It was one of those gauzy looking things women wore because they thought it hid everything well. With Grace, it clung to every curve of her deliciously round body. That is, when she was standing still. When she broke into that brisk, sexy walk of hers, it floated around her legs, billowing out with every step. The sunny yellow intensified the red of her hair and the golden hue of her skin.

Once again, he found himself enjoying her scent. Her perfume reminded him of tangled sheets, glistening bodies. It also reminded him he hadn't had sex in awhile. That had to explain why he could not seem to stop thinking about this woman.

"Was there something you needed? There isn't anything wrong with the house, is there?" she asked, her voice floating back to him.

"No, I was just wondering what people do for excitement in Cannon on Friday night," he said, cursing himself again. *Why the hell did I come here?*

He usually had no problem keeping himself occupied, but this was Cannon, and he didn't have his cable hooked up. That was the only reason he was over here. He had no ESPN, and it was driving him crazy.

It had nothing to do with her or her gorgeous, curly auburn hair. Jesus, she had a lot of hair. Even though she had tried to secure the mass of curls at the base of her neck, he could tell it probably reached half way down her back. What would it feel like draped across his abdomen, following the same path as her lips while she moved lower...?

"Well, usually there's a football game," she said, fortunately breaking his fantasy. "But they're out of town this week. You can go to The Well. It is likely to be a rowdy night and you might be able to make a few arrests. The problem you may have there is it's college night and they let seventeen and older in. What ever it is, it can't be any worse than one of Peterson's Mary Tyler Moore Parties."

"Mary Tyler Moore Parties?"

She stopped again and he ran into her, once more causing the same little bolts of awareness to skitter across his skin and her scent to fill his senses. When she turned and faced him, he noticed a single curl had escaped her ribbon tied hair. He itched to put it back in its place—or pull that ribbon and let it all fall down, just to see exactly what it looked like unbound.

He jammed both of his hands in the pocket of his jeans.

"Dr. Peterson, along with the inedible cuisine his wife cooks, has a tendency to give the worst parties. You know, like Mary Tyler Moore. I'm always amazed we don't find a dead body by the end." She crossed her arms beneath her breast and cocked her head to side. The single curl danced in the air. "You're probably wondering why I'm standing here babbling."

"Well, being the well trained police officer that I am, I'd have to deduce you didn't want to go."

She made a face. "I really don't."

When she didn't turn to leave, he couldn't help but ask, "Why do you go then?"

"I owe Dr. Peterson, and I respect him. Plus, he's the head of the department."

"Well, I guess I'll hit Zeno's then," he said. Ms. Janey and Barney-the-deputy had both assured him this was the best pizza place in town.

"I envy you," Grace said. "What I wouldn't do for one of their pizzas with everything on it, plus extra cheese."

"I'll tell you what. If you get home at a decent hour..." he said and raised an eyebrow when she snorted. "...come on over for a piece of pizza and a beer."

The moment he said the words, he wanted to call them back. He had to be losing his mind. Why the hell had he invited her? Half of him hoped she would refuse. The other half hoped she'd jump his bones right there in her front yard. The only answer was that he was deranged. Inviting her over would be the epitome of torture. She was a woman to whom he was attracted—but who he knew was completely wrong for him—and he'd just condemned himself to spending more time in her presence. By his own invitation, no less.

She stared at him for a moment, her eyes widened with surprise. Then a knowing look, with a hint of amusement, lightened them. It was if she sensed he'd twisted himself into a predicament. Her lips curved just slightly. "You're on. I'll be there with bells on by eight."

She walked down the sidewalk. As he stood there, wondering what had just gotten into him, he could not help but admire that exquisite ass. Because the material of her dress was light and didn't cling, he could just make out a vague outline of each cheek.

He sighed and walked across the street, thinking of his bizarre behavior toward his landlady. Ren made a point of avoiding entanglements and never had a problem before meeting Grace, but there was something in her that drew him. There was a throb of anticipation mixed with dread beating in his heart—not to mention more throbbing in other places further south. *That's it,* he decided. *If she does show up, I'll just cut the evening short somehow.*

The scary thing was, he really didn't want to.

℘℃℧

Grace stood in the kitchen, talking to Lorna Peterson and Dr. Homer Gump. Dr. Gump was one of the "bachelor professors" she'd befriended after returning to Cannon. Round and short, he measured just over five feet. A few wisps of hair covered his bald head. The coke-bottle glasses he'd worn for years emphasized his bright blue eyes.

He specialized in American history, and his passion was General George Washington. His fascination bordered on obsession in Grace's opinion, but he was such a sweet little man, she just couldn't help showing interest.

He and Dr. Myers lived together, and both seemed content to remain bachelors. Since both were past retirement age, Grace figured that was a given. Julia was convinced they were living in sin. Grace had decided she just didn't want to think about it.

"Jason told me you're making some progress in your research, Grace," Lorna Peterson said, trying to tame Gump's tongue.

"Yes," Grace said, smiling.

Somewhere in her early sixties, Lorna Peterson still held onto the slim figure that had made her a beauty queen years earlier. The mother of three boys, all historians, she had a natural tendency to mother everyone in the department. She refused to give in to the idea that she had to color her short gray hair, and Grace knew she would never consider surgery to hide the signs of aging. Of course, her alabaster skin showed very little age. Grace admired her for her loving nature and the fact that she could live with Dr. Peterson, who, like a lot of historians, could be single-minded in their studies.

Lorna nodded, showing her interest, and Grace continued, "I've been given a diary that may help a lot. If my assumptions are correct, the oldest daughter of Cord McPherson wrote it. It has a lot of great information. I plan on spending tomorrow going over it."

"Oh, my. That must be very exciting," Mrs. Peterson said. "You historians always find out the most interesting information, but you have to wade through so much to find it. I don't know how you do it. Sometimes I have to physically search the library for Jason."

Grace spent the next few minutes discussing the Cannon family and her assumptions. When she found an easy way to end the conversation, she smiled at Mrs. Peterson and thanked her for her drink.

As she walked away, she heard Dr. Gump expounding on the greatness of Washington's military expertise. A twinge of guilt nipped at her conscience for leaving Mrs. Peterson trapped—but not enough to rescue her. She stopped by the refreshment table and picked up a plate, thanking God that Mrs. Peterson had put out some appetizers that were not boiled.

"You know, Grace," Darian drawled behind her. "You really shouldn't eat so much cheese. It has a lot of saturated fat in it."

She sighed and turned to face him. "First of all, I really don't think it's any of your business. You gave up the right to criticize my eating habits several years ago. Besides," she said, popping a piece of hot pepper-jack in her mouth. "I haven't had anything to eat today but a bowl of oatmeal and coffee. I am hot, tired, and really not in the mood for you."

With that wonderful exit line, she turned and started to walk toward the patio doors to say her goodnights to the other professors. It was seven-thirty and she was ready to leave.

"I didn't think you would hold a grudge this long, Grace," Darian said, loud enough for people around them to hear. "It's been over five years since you left UT."

"You knew Dr. Michaels at UT?" Dr. Proctor, the widower asked, his green eyes alight with curiosity. "I had no idea you knew each other."

She cringed at the interested tone. Dr. Arnold Proctor was forever trying to set her up with men. Last year he thought Deputy Barney would be a good choice.

"Oh, yes," Darian said. "Grace and I dated for awhile when she taught at UT."

"Oh, then you must be excited getting to teach together again," Dr. Meyers said. "Grace really does have a flair for teaching the Old West. Why, just yesterday I heard a couple of students talking about her lecture on the first Presidential election in Texas."

Grace's face heated. She decided enough was enough. "Really, I'm happy about Dr. Dawson teaching here, and I really appreciate the dinner, Mrs. Peterson," she said. "But I have another engagement tonight."

Once again she tried to make an exit. She grabbed her purse off of the kitchen counter and hurried to the front door.

"I'll escort you to your car," Darian offered.

"I walked," she said without turning around.

"Then I really feel the need to see you home personally, Grace."

He followed her, closing door behind him and nipping at her heels like a Pomeranian.

"Look, Darian," she said, turning to face him and settling her hands on her hips. "I'm not in the mood tonight, okay? This isn't a big city. There hasn't been a murder here since Gina Fowler found her husband in bed with her sister, and that was thirty years ago. So, please, I really don't need your assistance tonight."

"I wouldn't feel comfortable with letting you walk home alone."

She grunted, trying to strangle the scream gathering in her throat, turned around, and started down the sidewalk.

"You really didn't need to pretend to have a date tonight," he said. "We could have made some excuse to be alone."

She didn't say anything, just kept walking, and increasing her stride. He sped up and caught up with her, grabbing her elbow. "I'm not sure I could find something decent to eat in this town. I do have a fine bottle of Merlot. I remember you like Merlot."

Grace sighed, pulled her arm free and resumed walking. "Listen, Darian. I really don't want to get together to talk about research or the good ol' days at UT." Sarcasm laced her voice. "I really do have plans tonight. Besides, I don't like Merlot, you do."

Relief poured through her when she stopped at the sidewalk leading to her front porch.

"You love Merlot, you told me," he said in a slightly whiny voice that reminded her of a three-year-old upset over losing a treat. She wouldn't have been surprised to see him stomp his foot and cross his arms. "We used to drink it all the time."

"Because *you* liked it, Darian." *Where the hell are my keys?*

"Then why did you drink it and tell me you liked it?" he asked.

"Because I was twenty-six, and I thought I was in love."

"We *were* in love."

She didn't laugh, but it was a close call. "No, we weren't. At least I know you weren't. If you were, I wouldn't have found you fucking Veronica on my desk."

"That is such a vulgar term." Disgust intermingled with shock in his voice.

"I call them as I see them." She turned away from him. "Really Darian, no need to walk me to my door."

He ignored her comment and followed her. "You know, if you would have tried to enjoy the physical side of our relationship more, I wouldn't have gone to Ronnie."

"Really? So it was my fault," she said. "Did you ever think it might have been your fault? Maybe the fact you thought I needed help in bed had something to do with you and your technique? That maybe there was something wrong with you?"

"No."

"Well, that about sums it up." She turned to face him. "I would say I had a great time, but it'd be a lie. Goodnight, Darian." She turned to leave and he grabbed her arm.

"I thought I could join you. You and I both know you don't have a date tonight."

"First of all, I'd rather be alone, dateless for the next twenty years than spend any extra time with you." She paused, yanking her arm away from him. "Second of all, I didn't say I had a date, I said I had a previous engagement."

She tried to turn again, but Darian grabbed her arm a little more forcefully, digging his fingers into her arm.

"Grace when are you going to give up this idiotic farce, and admit that you don't have anything to do tonight? When I set this up with Dr. Peterson, I thought that you and I could spend some time together, maybe work through our problems."

Was he dense?

"No." She jerked her arm to get him to release it. He moved to grab her arm again, and she backed away, her nerves jumping to life at the anger simmering in his cold eyes.

"I really think you need to leave the lady alone," a familiar male voice said.

Chapter Four

Ren stood at the bottom of the stairs to Grace's porch, holding a very freaking hot pizza box and a six-pack of Bud. At first, fury had churned inside his stomach and rose violently to almost choke him. Then he realized he had no right to be angry. The anger dissolved and he reminded himself Grace was not Delta, the bitch, his ex-wife. They weren't even dating. They were just friendly. *In a completely non-sexual kind of way,* he told himself.

Well, at least during the waking hours. Last night, he had awakened, his heart threatening to jump out of his chest and sweat rolling down his back, his arousal pretty evident under the sheets. He'd spent more than twenty minutes in a cold shower and still had a hard-on that could've hammered a nine-inch spike into concrete. He'd finally had to take matters into his own hands, so to speak.

He shook himself free of the memories to deal with the present. He'd returned from picking up the pizza and beer to find her talking to a tall blond man dressed in an expensive suit in front of her house. It was really none of his business and he knew it. He should even be there, and he knew that, too. He'd decided to bring the pizza back to her house, rather than wait and see if she'd show up at his place. That way, he could leave when he wanted, he told himself, and not be saddled with some bothersome woman.

Neither Grace nor her companion had noticed him upon his approach, but when the guy had grabbed Grace's arm a second time and with a little more force than necessary, Ren had decided to step in. *Acting as the new chief of police, of course,* he thought.

The blond man turned, his pale blue eyes surprised by the interruption. "I really don't think Grace is in need of any help," he said.

"Oh, but you see, I'm her previous engagement," Ren said. "I'd appreciate it if you would move the fuck out of my way so we could go inside and eat."

The use of profanity had the desired affect. The blond man's lips flattened and his eyes narrowed. Ren shifted his attention to Grace.

"Grace, honey, this pizza is hot. Could you move that cute ass of yours?" Her lips quirked once and her eyes twinkled.

"Sure thing, Ren." She turned to the blond. "As you can see, I'm busy tonight."

"I'll stop by tomorrow so we can talk about your new research," the man said, not giving up even as he walked down the sidewalk. Grace's spine straightened, but she ignored the comment.

She turned to face Ren with a smile so brilliant he blinked, stunned momentarily. "Thanks," she said. "I thought he wouldn't go away."

"You're welcome," he replied, and then they stood there facing each other, crickets chirping in the nearby hedges, with her smiling at him almost shyly. "You know, this pizza really is fucking hot."

"Oh." Her eyes widened. "Let me put Sam out and then you can come in." A round of barking started when she said the name, but she didn't move. She just kept staring at him with those whiskey eyes.

"Grace."

"Yes?" Her voice slipped an octave. The sound of it glided over his skin, sending another wave of heat blasting through him.

He let out an aggravated sigh. "Pizza," he said. "Hot. Burning my hand."

"Oh." Her face flushed again. He realized her blushes were cute and, for some unknown reason, arousing as hell. "Umm...yeah...I'll be right back." And with that, she slipped inside and the barking stopped.

ℰↄ℃ℛ

Grace gave Sam as much attention as she could as she herded him out the back door, telling herself she'd feel guilty about it later. Once again thankful she hadn't been at home enough to make a mess of her house, she opened the door. Ren he rushed passed her, asking where the kitchen was.

"Off to your left." He plopped the pizza carton on the small in front of a bay window looking out onto the street.

"Damn, that was hot," he said, shaking his hand.

"I'm sorry about Darian. He can a bit of pain." She grabbed a couple of plates from the cabinet and set them on the table. "You need a mug for the beer?"

"Nope."

"I have to get into something a little more comfortable, if you don't mind."

"No, I'll just make myself at home," he said with a crooked smile and those cute wrinkles crinkling around his chocolate eyes.

The look was so boyishly handsome, her stomach flip-flopped. He was gorgeous as the big bad sheriff, but he was deadly with that smile.

She hurried down the hall to her room. Once she closed the door, she drew in a deep breath. She had never thought he would show up here. Heated pleasure still tingled down her spine as she remembered the sound of his voice when he had appeared. Dark and dangerous. Someone like him had never been her type, but, oh, she wanted that to be her type now. She could just imagine his husky tenor groaning her name.

She took a deep breath and shook her head, trying to push away the image of him in her bed. Preferably handcuffed to the headboard.

Thank God the rest of the house did not look like her room. It had taken her at least ten minutes that morning to find a pair of stockings or pantyhose without a hole or run and another ten to find a pair of heels. There were shoes strewn all over the floor while the soon-to-be-garbage hose littered her unmade bed. She pulled her dress over her head, and threw it on top of everything else on her bed. Then she pulled on an old pair of jeans and a Cannon College T-shirt, and headed back to the kitchen.

She found Ren already eating pizza. The dainty little table at which he sat looked like something from a Parisian café. With his height and his massive build, he appeared two times too big to be sitting at it. A zing of heat warmed her tummy and slid down between her legs. When she moved, she swore her panties were already wet.

Ren watched as she filled her plate and grabbed a beer. "I have to thank you once again for saving me from starvation," she said. She popped the top of the can and took a large swig, not caring if it was unladylike. She deserved it. "Oh, I needed that."

He stared at her a moment or two as he tried to figure out what was wrong with the picture. He assumed wouldn't she even go for the beer, and if she had, she'd grab a mug. He definitely did not expect her to chug it like a frat boy. On top of that, she dressed like a twenty-year-old coed. Her worn jeans hugged her thighs, hips and butt. The white T-shirt she wore showed its age, with several places transparent enough to allow him a little glimpse at her lacy bra. The soft swell of her breasts was visible through the thin cotton fabric.

His blood thickened and his body temperature spiked. He breathed deeply and with an unbelievable amount of control, brought his focus back to the conversation.

"So, you want to tell me about your admirer?" Ren asked casually.

"Darian Daniel Dawson. Super PhD. He's going to be teaching here for a semester. And he's not an admirer. He's an ex-fiancé."

She bit into her slice of pizza, and hummed. Literally hummed with pleasure. Every thought disintegrated at the sound. A slow roll of heat spread to his groin. His balls tightened as he imagined her humming while holding his cock in her mouth.

"Peterson arm-wrestled him into teaching next semester while he's researching in the area," she said. "How much of the conversation did you hear?"

"Not much. From about the point you mentioned a woman named Veronica." He shifted, trying to ease the tightness in his jeans.

She grimaced. "Great. I really don't want it to get around. If you don't mind."

Ren shifted again, causing another groan of protest from the insubstantial chair. He couldn't find a comfortable way to sit in the little dainty thing, and worried it could not hold his weight. It was in danger of collapsing with each move, and to make matters worse, he slid around more, watching Grace.

The woman took eating to a whole other level. Taking another bite, she sucked a long piece of cheese into her mouth, humming the entire time, her eyes closed in ecstasy. Okay, so the ecstasy had nothing to do with him, but still, it didn't help the churning lust in his gut. If she didn't stop humming and sucking on that cheese, he was going to have another long night of cold showers. *Women should only sound like that during sex, not while they're eating. It should be illegal.*

She opened her eyes and looked at him expectantly. *What the hell were we talking about?* Something about the guy on her porch. Yeah, the ex-fiance.

"Ex-fiancé?" he asked.

"Yes. We were engaged when I taught at UT."

"Is he the only one or are there others?" And why the hell was he so interested?

"Nope. Just the one. And seeing how that was my one and only proposal, and that was six years ago, I don't see myself getting married anytime soon."

"Not a lot of prospects in Cannon?"

"Well, every now and then maybe another professor asks me out."

"You don't go out with any hometown guys, I take it?"

"I didn't date much in high school, being the nerd that I am." A self-depreciating smile lit her face. "But most of those guys have been married at least once. They come with a lot of baggage. It's that or I'm a distant relation. That's one thing about living in a small town. Plus, I've known some of them so long I can't take any of them seriously. Unfortunately, Dr. Proctor has taken an interest in me. Want another slice?"

"Sure."

She plopped another piece down on his plate.

"Who's Dr. Proctor?"

"He's one of the other history professors. He's driving me crazy."

"Crazy, how?" he asked. Was he going to have to threaten this guy, too?

"He's about seventy years old, with nothing else to do outside of his garden and his lectures."

"Isn't he a little old for you?"

She chuckled. "No. I mean he keeps trying to fix me up. At first, I didn't realize what he was up to. He seems to think I need help romantically, so he takes it on himself to find me dates. Most of the time, the guys have no idea what is going on. The first time he tried it, it was the new accounting professor a couple of years ago. He told him I was being audited to get him interested. Since then, there have been many, many disasters. Just this summer he tried to fix me up with Barney. Told him someone was stalking me."

"My deputy, Barney?"

"Yep."

"My deputy?" Ren asked again. "Who has to be, what, at least six years younger than you?"

"Some men like older women."

He snorted.

"No need to get insulting." The prissy tone crept back in her voice. And, God help him, it turned him on. All he could envision was Grace wearing nothing but a smile and holding a ruler.

"I'm not. But he's a kid, no matter what his age is." And what Grace needed was a man. An image of Grace entwined in the arms of some stranger burst into his mind before he could prevent it. His chest burned with some unknown emotion and he rubbed it, trying to ease the irritation.

"Yeah, well, avoid Dr. Proctor. He'll be trying to fix you..." she said pointing at Ren. "...up with me..." She pointed a thumb at her chest. "...in no time. It's really kind of sweet in a way. He was married for over forty years, but they never had any children. He has sort of adopted me and apparently thinks I'm his only hope for grandchildren."

"You don't want to be fixed up with me?" he asked, feeling a little put out that she seemed revolted by the idea. Okay, so he didn't want to want her, but it irritated him that she might not be as attracted to him as he was to her.

"I really don't have time to get serious right now," she replied. "I'm researching an idea for a book, and it takes up a lot of my free time. Plus, you have to admit we're not what you would call compatible. You can't say I'm your type."

He decided to ignore that comment. "You don't date?"

"Date who? You're the best prospect to hit Cannon in about ten years and I'm sure I impressed you." A flush crept up from her neck and then her face. He didn't know if it was because she had named him as a prospect, or the memory of what had happened the day before.

"Well, I'm not sure what you mean about that," he told her. "It was one of the friendliest welcomes I've ever had."

Her faced turned an even brighter shade of red, but she smiled. "Yeah, well, the only man in my life right now is Sam, and he's been fixed."

"That says something about your personal life."

"Yeah, it about sums up my success with men," she said with a grin. "Besides, Mom told me you had just gotten divorced recently. I figured anyone who had gone through something like that would probably steer clear of any kind of commitment."

His humor faded. The same anger rose and he fought to gain control of his emotions. The silence stretched to an uncomfortable length.

She cleared her throat. "I'm sorry. I'm not the prying type and I was just making a statement of fact. I just wanted to let you know Professor Proctor might bombard you. This way you've been warned."

Some of the bitterness that had been choking him dissolved. He tried to smile. "Okay."

"So, what made you want to come to a small town like Cannon?"

"Sick of the game. I got sick of fighting the system to keep the bad guys in jail long enough to make a difference. And," he said, getting another piece of pizza. "To get ahead, you had to kiss a lot of ass. Not my kind of thing."

Her lips curved into closed mouth smile that sent a straight jolt of lust to his dick. "Yeah, somehow I sensed that about you."

శిుౖౖ

Gabriel Michaels let out a frustrated sigh. The revisions for his latest thriller weren't going as planned. Normally, unlike a lot of writers, he loved this process of the game. Of shaping the work, making it spectacular. But something, no *someone*, was keeping him from working. His concentration was shot, and one leggy brunette was to blame. The ringing of his phone broke his concentration.

"Hello?"

"Gabriel? This is Julia."

"Hey, Jules," he said, knowing the cool voice as soon as she spoke. It was the voice that haunted his dreams and heated his blood. He had to be a masochist. "What's up?"

"I think you need to make a trip to Cannon."

His heart skipped a beat. "Miss me?" he said, hoping he was right.

"Not really," she said. "But the Triple D showed up in town last night. He is apparently staying through the semester. I think Grace could use some backup. It was either you or your folks. And although I love them, she would kill me if I called them, and they showed up and parked the RV out in front of her house."

"Yeah," he said with a smile, and then scowled when he thought about that bastard bothering his sister, Grace. "What the hell is the jerk doing there in Cannon anyway?"

"I'm not sure, but Grace is always a pushover, you know that. I don't want him to hurt her again. Then I'd have to kill him. This being Texas, I'm sure I'd end up on death row. Unless I could hide the body. My father does own some land west of town."

"Well," Gabriel said slowly, thinking of the deadline for the revisions for his new book. "I guess I could make it into town in a few days. Don't tell her I'm coming though."

"Okay, thanks. I hope I didn't interrupt your Friday night frolicking, but I was really worried about her."

"What do you mean, Friday night frolicking?" he asked. His doorbell rang and he went up to answer it. "I was working on some revisions due in next week."

He opened the door, and found "Kandy-with-a-K", his neighbor at the door.

"Hi, Gabe, honey, I brought some cookies I baked over for you," she said, with a seductive smile.

She was average height with big blonde hair, big blue eyes, and big fake breasts. He cursed the two-week affair they'd had last summer when he had been bored.

Okay, strike that. The two-week affair he had because he had spent a frustrating month in Julia's company while visiting Grace. He had to prove to himself that big-boobed blondes, whose main objective in life was to look good, were still his type of women. Even with her standing there smiling at him, her breasts almost completely hanging out her shirt, he felt more interested in the cookies she offered than the sex that she considered the main meal.

"You sound busy, Gabe, honey," Julia said with deadly sweetness. "Just be here next week for your sister," she warned, and hung up.

Irritated, he tossed his phone on a nearby chair. Lately, they didn't seem to be able to have a conversation without fighting.

"Is there something wrong, Gabe?"

Kandy's sugary sweet tone cut into his thoughts. When he finally focused on her, his body stirred. It was hard not to because the woman was gorgeous. No man in his right mind would say otherwise.

He smiled reassuringly and pulled the door open wider to allow her to enter. "No, nothing really."

She held up the plate of cookies. "Are you interested?"

The double meaning wasn't lost on him. He took the cookies and placed them on his desk as he took her hand to lead her back to the bedroom. Even knowing how disappointing the sex was the last go round didn't stop his body from reacting to the invitation. Within moments they were on the bed, his pants undone, and her hand expertly gliding over his erection. He closed his eyes as she kissed down his throat, to his chest, leading down his body.

Her tongue brushed over his cock. He threaded his fingers through her hair as his mind drifted to another woman, one who drove him insane. Kandy's fingers slipped to his balls as his mind created the fantasy that it was Julia's hands, her mouth. Disgust filled him when he realized he was using Kandy to take out his frustration with Julia. Again. No matter how much his body pulsed with need, he gently pushed her shoulders. She smiled up at him and for half a second, he thought, *what the hell?* Kandy probably didn't give a damn. She only came to him when she wanted a quick fuck, but the dissatisfaction he'd felt during their affair welled up.

"Sorry, babe, I just can't."

Her smile faded. She gave his hard-on a speaking glance then said, "You have a funny way of showing it."

"It's just not what I should be doing."

"Oh, and what should you be doing? It's not like we haven't before."

"I..." How did he say this without sounding like a total jackass? Which he admittedly was. "Listen, I was thinking of someone else, and it just isn't fair to you."

She stood, taking a few moments to readjust her clothes. Even after making the decision, his dick twitched as she smoothed her hand over her breasts. When she looked at him, a mixture of pity and irritation darkened her eyes.

"You know what your problem is, Gabe? You take yourself too seriously. It was just a way to relieve the tension." She shrugged. "I can find someone else to help me if you're too stupid to take me up on my offer."

"I'm—"

She held up her hand. "Please, spare me. I don't need your excuses or your apologies. If you think that I can't find another fuck buddy, you have another think coming."

With that parting shot, she turned and marched out of his bedroom, slamming his front door. He relieved the tension she'd created within moments and was back at his desk. His mind drifted back to his conversation with Julia as he reached for a cookie. It was then he realized Kandy had taken the whole damn plate with her. Not that he could blame her.

Sighing in disappointment, Gabe's thoughts turned to his sister and that asshole, Dawson. He couldn't do anything about what happened several years ago, but he would make damn sure if the bastard tried anything now, he would pay.

Darian Daniel Dawson would think twice before trying to hurt another woman. Gabriel would see to that. He couldn't wait to hear him cry like a girl.

Chapter Five

Grace's eyes crossed from exhaustion. She closed them and set the diary she'd been studying in her lap. She sat on the loveseat in her office, all cozy beneath her grandmother's handmade quilt. After spending most of her Saturday morning reading over Suzanna Cannon's diary, Grace had come to one conclusion. The woman was a bitch.

She sighed as tension knotted her neck. Carefully, she slid the ninety-year-old book back into its protective covering. She thought about Suzanna and her plight in life, watching her younger sisters marry, being forced to stay and take care of her father, who had been a bitter, hateful man. Grace would be a bitch after spending a week taking care of her father and she loved him to pieces. Suzanna hadn't been so lucky.

She stretched and groaned as her back muscles, cramped from bending over a book for hours, protested. Sam looked up at her, irritated that she'd awakened him from his nap.

"I'll tell you what. We'll go see the bachelors."

His tail thumped at the familiar phrase. He jumped up with a woof and ran toward the front door. Minutes later they were heading to the professor's home, Sam on his leash and Grace dressed in a pair of old jeans and a sweatshirt.

As she turned the corner of Oak Street, she noticed a new model BMW make a U-turn in the middle of the street. She sighed, irritation creeping down her spine. Darian loved "Beamers" and leased a new one each year. She groaned and increased her stride. She'd hoped he'd taken her not-so-subtle hint to leave her the hell alone last night, but for some reason, she had a sinking feeling he wouldn't. She heard a car door slam and knew he was hot on her heels.

"Gracie, I tried to catch you at home but you had gone. You're lucky I saw you heading this way," he said, walking fast to keep up with her. She glanced at him. His face was ruddy from the west Texas wind.

Darian stopped when Sam bared his teeth. He looked down at the dog, and a trace of anger flashed in his cool blue eyes.

"Where did you find this one, Grace? He looks like some kind of mongrel."

Sam's menacing growl grew louder, and the hair on his back stood on end. Darian took a step back. Grace did her damnedest not to smile, but failed.

"I have a lot of work to do today." She loosened the slack of Sam's leash just a tad to allow him to crowd Darian a little more. "And plans for tonight. So if you'll excuse—"

"What, plans with that local yokel who tried to intimidate me last night? I could have that man's job if I wanted to."

"Listen, Darian, no one gives a damn if you are one of the Virginia Dawsons. They really don't care you *are* the reigning weenie on campus. So, if you start trying to throw your weight around in this town, you really could find yourself in trouble. Besides, my plans are with Julia. She said something about castration when I told her you were in town, so I wouldn't show your head, no pun intended, around my house tonight."

"Really, Grace, you seem to have lost all refinement living here. You say the most vulgar things."

"That's what I'm like now." She turned and started walking again. She raised her voice so she didn't have to turn and look at the idiot. "I'm thinking about chunking my job at the college, moving into a trailer and becoming a stripper. I may even get a tattoo." She looked over her shoulder to find him standing on the corner of Oak and Burnett with his mouth hanging open.

℘○℃

Dr. Meyers and Dr. Gump lived in a small little cape cod surrounded by several live oaks. Their yard was a showcase to hard work. Being that it was October, their mums were in full bloom. Along the borders, they'd planted yellow pansies that would probably flower until the first freeze, if they had one this year. Next door, where Dr. Proctor lived, there was no sign of life and his car was gone. She strolled up the walk and knocked on their door, and had to shush Sam when he started barking.

Dr. Meyers answered. Grace always had to tip her head back slightly to look him in the eye. He was about six-foot-five, with long gray hair he usually tied into a ponytail. He forever wore some kind of tie-dyed shirt when he wasn't teaching. Today, he'd chosen his rainbow shirt, which he wore with a pair of worn blue jeans. He smiled as soon as he saw it was her and Sam who had landed on his doorstep.

"Grace," he said, opening the screen door for her. "Come on in, you two. I was just doing a little reading."

Grace and Sam walked into the house, but Dr. Meyers' attention was focused down the sidewalk. His smile faded slightly.

"Is that Dawson?"

"Yes. He followed me here."

He shut the door and trailed Grace into the kitchen. She plopped down on one of the bar stools at the counter of the island and Sam sprawled on his favorite place in the kitchen—in front of the refrigerator. She sighed and allowed the tension to drain out of her limbs. These confrontations with Darian were really starting to get stressful.

"I just made some sweet tea. Would you like a drink?" He pulled a couple of glasses out of the cupboard when she nodded. He set the tea in front of her. "Homer's out back, puttering around his tomatoes."

He studied her for a second and his eyes lost all their humor. "Grace, I know this may not be kosher, but I really don't like Dawson. There's something about him I do not trust."

"Well, that just means you have good instincts, Dr. Meyers," Grace said, smiling at his protective tone. Out of the three professors, he was the most grounded. Dr. Gump and Dr. Proctor were intelligent and knew more in their fields of study than she would probably ever know in hers. But both reminded her of the stereotypical absent-minded professor. Although she had to remind Dr. Meyers to take his medications and that he had his bifocal glasses on his head, he was pretty good at dealing with every day life. "He is the dreaded ex-fiancé."

"Oh," he said sympathetically. "Well, I don't like him on principal now."

Grace smiled at him. "You know, Dr. Meyers, I have to marry you. Not only do you make the best sweet tea in this county, but also you stand behind me in my decisions. If you won't marry me, I don't care. Come live in sin at my house."

He smiled. "I think our main problem with living in sin is that you won't call me Fredrick. That, and I'm old enough to be your grandfather."

Grace laughed and gave him a hug. "I know you think it's silly, but I can't bring myself to call you by your first name. You were my first instructor here at Cannon."

"How's the reading going?" he asked, refilling her glass.

"Okay." She thought about the tone of the diary and descriptions written by Suzanna. "I've come to one conclusion after reading the first forty pages or so. She really didn't like anyone."

Dr. Meyers let out a bark of a laugh. "From what I hear, she was a bitch."

"I was trying to be nice," Grace said with mock condemnation in her voice.

"Yeah, but she's dead and buried with no known relatives in town. I promise I won't tell a soul."

"Yeah, well, you're right. She was a bitch." She got up and set her empty glass by the sink. "But then, who could blame her? She was stuck taking care of Willie Cannon, who didn't have the nicest personality. You know, though, I'm not so sure there aren't a few of her relatives left around."

"Really? I thought neither Millicent nor Suzanna had children."

"There was a middle sister who no one talks about but she was mentioned in some newspaper articles." Grace leaned against the counter and supported herself on her elbows. "Her name was Charlotte and she moved south after she married. According to Suzanna, she had two children before she died. The funny thing is that she isn't mentioned in any of the official records at the courthouse. I would have remembered a third sister. It may have to do with the way she died."

Dr. Meyers lifted an eyebrow and she continued.

"There's some indication that she committed suicide. The problem is that all of this information comes from Suzanna. I mean, she recorded all kinds of things in that journal, and most of them were probably true. They just weren't the kind of things that I would put in *my* diary. Anyway," she said, "I need to find her sister's married name. I have her maiden name, of course, so at least that's a start."

"If you could find her children or grandchildren, that would certainly help," he said. "They might be able to tell you whether or not Cordelia Cannon had actually dressed as a man and robbed banks under the name of Cord McPherson." He paused thoughtfully. "But maybe they wouldn't want anyone to know."

"Why not?" Grace asked. "I think it would be intriguing to have a little scandal like that. The best we have in my family are some moon-shiners on Dad's side and Great-Uncle Bart who liked to wear dresses."

"Not all people would be happy about that, you know," he said, his voice inflecting more of the upper crust Boston accent than usual. "That is just not accepted in some circles, darling."

Grace laughed. "Well, maybe so. Hopefully, they won't think that way."

Heavy footsteps sounded on the back porch and then the kitchen door opened. Homer Gump was probably close to one hundred pounds overweight. While Dr. Meyers exuded East Coast sophistication, Dr. Gump always looked like he needed a good tailor and an even better iron for his clothes. His round little face broke into a radiant smile when he saw their visitors. He bent down to give Sam a pet. "Grace," he said, his German accent lacing his voice. "Look at these beauties!"

He held out a basket almost overflowing with tomatoes. "These fall tomatoes are always the best, and with this warm front, it has given them a little reprieve. You'll have to take some home, yes, yes."

"Don't worry, I will," she said. "Julia is coming over tonight. I'd love to have a few for a salad."

"Done." Dr. Gump set the basket on the counter and pulling a smaller basket out from the bottom cabinet. "Now I want to warn you that Dr. Proctor, bless his romantic soul, is going to try to fix you up with this Dr. Daniel."

Grace watched him go through the tomatoes, inspecting each, picking the best for her, and she smiled. "It's Dr. Dawson, and it won't do him any good. He's my ex-fiancé."

"Mmm, I knew I didn't like him on sight. He is too slick to be a history professor."

"Homer," Dr. Meyers said with a hint of warning in his voice. Grace knew the only one who control Dr. Gump's tongue was Dr. Meyers.

Dr. Gump grumbled as he placed the basket of tomatoes in front of Grace. "Well, that doesn't mean I have to like him."

Grace smiled at his defense, and walked over to him. She leaned down, gave him a kiss on the cheek, and a hug.

"You really are the sweetest man," she said, making him blush.

&OCR

By nine o'clock that evening, Grace was sure that she was feeling no pain. In fact, she was sure she couldn't feel her legs. Julia had shown up a few hours earlier with the ingredients for her nachos and a bottle of tequila. They had started off with margaritas, but Grace had pulled out some limes and they had both started to do a shot or two of straight tequila. Her favorite disco CD, *ABBA's Greatest Hits*, blared on the stereo. Grace was sprawled on the sofa and Julia sat in her overstuffed chair.

"You know, Grace, you should go after this police chief guy." Julia licked the salt off her hand, gulped down the shot of Cuervo Gold, and sucked on the lime.

"No, he's not my type," Grace said.

"What do you mean? You have a type?"

"Yeah, and long-legged movie star good looks are not it." Even if she had dreamed of him last night.

"Why not? What have you got against studs?" Julia asked.

Grace giggled, picked up the tequila, and poured them both another shot.

"Listen, I wouldn't mind having my own personal stud-muffin, but you know how they look at me. I'm their drinking buddy, their pal who tells them how to meet my friend, the tall brunette with the green eyes."

Julia rolled her green eyes as Grace glanced pointedly in her direction.

"You remember that cute accounting professor?" Grace asked. "He said kissing me was like kissing his sister. How do you fight that argument?" She licked her hand, swigged the tequila, and sucked the lime. "Besides, I gave up on passion years ago. I'm not the type of woman who inspires poetry." She sighed when Julia looked at her as if she had grown another head. "I'm sure that some day I'll settle down, but I'm just not that passionate in bed. I told you. Still, what I wouldn't give for Ben Affleck to show up at my door and tell me he just wanted to use me for sex."

Julia made a humming sound of pleasure. He was one of her favorites, too. "Sex with Ben, with or without commitment, that would be a dream come true. I would die a happy woman after a week of that. Well, maybe a week or two," she said.

The ring of the doorbell brought Sam, who'd abandoned them after they finished the nachos, out of his bedroom in a frenzy of barking. His eighty-pound body quivered with excitement at the possibility of an intruder, or another human bearing food. It took several moments for Julia to get past him and to the door, only to find Darian standing on her porch illuminated by a weak pool of light.

Sam butted his head forward, trying to shove Grace out of the way and push the screen door open. She grabbed the dog by the collar and stepped in front of Julia. Stars circled in front of her eyes and her head spun because of her quick movements and the tequila.

"What are you doing here?" she asked, shaking her head to clear it.

"I told you that I was going to come over tonight," Darian said, looking past her with a sour look toward Julia. "I see you haven't improved from last night's companion."

Grace sighed as Julia called Darian a particularly ugly name. It had been going so well up until then.

ဆဝဘ

Ren sat in his favorite chair—his *only* chair, in fact—that had been delivered along with the rest of his household that day, and started emptying boxes. No matter how many times he moved, he could always feel at home once he had everything unpacked. It was something his mother had instilled in him throughout their years of moving from post to post. Any place was home as long as you had your family and your favorite things with you. *Well,* he thought. *At least I still have my things.*

He hadn't brooded over his divorce for a long time, and he didn't feel particularly depressed today, but moving into a house left him a little uneasy. He'd moved to an apartment after the divorce, living out of boxes for months until the opportunity opened up in Cannon. A house was bigger, emptier than a small apartment.

He stood, walked to one of the front windows, and looked across the street. He'd seen a little red convertible sitting outside of Grace's house for the last few hours and thought it may have been Dawson's. Glancing at the clock, he realized that it was close to ten. He wondered if she'd changed her mind about her ex-fiancé. A little flashy car like that seemed right up the bastard's alley. Not that it was any of Ren's business. He just didn't think Grace was that stupid.

As he was about to turn away, he noticed a BMW slowly drive past her house and park, facing the wrong way, in front. The ex-fiancé stepped out of the car and walked up the front path to Grace's door. That woman had to be stupid inviting a loser like him to her house. Ren had heard her comment about Veronica and wondered how someone could forgive something like that. He knew he would never be able to forgive his ex-wife or ex-best friend for what they had done to him.

He narrowed his eyes when the sound of raised voices reached him. The man was still standing on her porch arguing with someone through the screen door. *Looks like I need to step in again,* he thought. *After all, I am the new Chief of Police.*

Chapter Six

Grace looked into Darian's cool blue eyes, wondering if there was some kind of history of mental illness in his family. As he angrily tried to convince her they needed to talk, she winced at the names Julia was throwing at him from behind. She struggled not to laugh at the little bulb of spit that had formed on Darian's mouth. Her head was spinning and she kept fighting the urge to tell Darian to go screw himself.

They'd really had too much to drink. They needed to eat some more. Those nachos hadn't gone that far. *Brownies sound really good about now.* She shook her head, trying to clear it of the enticing images of food.

"Look," she said cutting both of them off. "This is a girl's night. No men. You aren't allowed to play here." She realized her speech was somewhat slurred and giggled. "So go play with yourself, Darian." Then she giggled again and clamped her hand over her mouth.

"Really, Grace, it seems I'm getting here just in time," he said. "Drinking to excess, using foul language, making vulgar comments. What has gotten into you?"

"About ten shots of tequila," she said, but it was muffled behind her hand.

"You know, this is getting to be old hat," Ren said from behind Darian.

"Darian was just leaving," Grace said sarcastically, as Darian turned to face Ren. *"Again.* Thanks for stopping by."

She hadn't heard Ren walk up, but then, she wasn't in top form. After ten shots of tequila, she probably would have missed an elephant coming up the sidewalk. He stood on the bottom step leading to her porch, but still seemed to tower over Darian. His plaid flannel shirt looked worn and soft from numerous washings, and his jeans looked as comfortable as the ones he had worn the day she met him. Warmth spread through her, licking at her hormones.

"Well, Chief, I see that the *girls* have started without you tonight," Darian said dryly. "No beer and pizza?"

"No, but you might want to move that Beamer," Ren replied, hooking his thumb toward Darian's car. "It's parked facing the wrong way. I just called it in and Barney's very efficient."

"Barney?"

"My deputy."

"It figures this town would have a Deputy named Barney," Darian said. "Well, we'll have this discussion at another time, Grace." He walked down the steps and hurried along the sidewalk to his car.

Ren chuckled to himself. The ex-fiancé didn't have a very manly walk. He turned back around. Grace leaned against the doorframe and gave him a sloppy smile. His warm blood heated to molten lava as she licked her lips. Her tongue darted out over her lower, fuller lip and he bit back a groan.

"Well, thank you again, Len Morello," she said as she opened the screen door in invitation. He accepted.

"That's Ren."

"That's what I said." She gave him a frown that caused a little wrinkle between her eyebrows. He curled his fingers into his palms to resist the urge to smooth it away.

She was wearing old sweat pants that, even though they fit loosely, seemed to hug every curve of her body. Her cropped top showed the barest hint of skin. He realized she wasn't wearing a bra beneath the shirt, and every movement she made caused her breasts to bounce or sway.

She'd freed her hair, and the mass of amber ringlets cascaded halfway down her back. Now he knew that his fantasies had been accurate. Ideas flashed before him—Grace on his bed, her hair a halo about her head, with a few rebellious curls dripping over her breasts, the puckered nipples peeking out. He shoved his hands in his pockets and hoped she was too drunk to notice his massive boner.

Her eyes dipped down, widened, and shot back up to his face. He felt the glance as if it'd been a lick. Fire coursed through him, and his reservations slowly melted away. He stepped forward, but she stayed him with her hand to his chest. Her lips tipped up in a mischievous smile.

"This is Goulia," she said, waving her hand behind her and smacking a gorgeous, leggy brunette in the chest. "I mean Julia."

He took a deep breath and hoped that some blood would seep back into his brain. "Nice to meet you," he said, making eye contact for a second and returning his gaze back to his drunk landlady.

"I take it you two have been drinking a little?" he asked. She nodded and turned, following her friend. He trailed them, his mind completely focused on her full, rounded ass.

Grace abruptly spun around, almost losing her balance, and put her fisted hands on her rounded hips. "No, Len," she said, looking serious again. "We has been drinking a lot. Are you going to take us in?" She walked backwards as Ren continued to walk forward.

Neither of them noticed the ottoman behind her. He didn't have time to react as she backed into it and lost her balance. She landed with a thump on the floor, on the other side of the ottoman. Julia laughed. Grace shot her a dirty look.

"That hurt."

He looked around the living room. He'd had a brief glance at it last night, and had noted the coziness. There was an overstuffed couch with a comfortable looking chair. They shared an end table with what looked like an antique lamp on it. Various shades of red and orange splashed throughout the room, from paintings on the wall to the throw rugs that covered the wooden floor. Two of the walls were lined with bookshelves filled to the brim with books. An antique dining table sat in front of the shelves, an ivory vase sat in the middle, holding a multitude of orange and red flowers.

Tonight it really did look like a private party for two had been going on. There were margarita and shot glasses littering the end tables, while the remnants of what looked like nachos sat on the floor in a huge bowl with two forks. The TV was blaring the beginning of a *Sex in the City* re-run and the stereo was playing something by ABBA.

Definitely a girl's night.

He held out his hand to Grace, since Julia was lying on the overstuffed red couch, still cackling. Grace took his hand and he pulled her up. Julia sat up, her short ebony hair sticking up in all different directions. "Sorry, but that was too funny, Grace."

"Yeah, well, if you'd fallen on your bony little ass, you would have been in a lot more pain than me," Grace replied, rubbing her rear end, trying to get rid of the sting. She turned to Ren and gave him a sensuous smile. He knew he'd be in trouble if she smiled at him like that when she was sober. "So, Len, we aren't going to be handcuffed and strip-searched?"

He stared at her for a second, trying to figure out if she was too drunk to make a sexual innuendo that blatant. The goofy smile on her face told him she had no idea what he was thinking. Images of Grace on his bed flashed in his mind, but this time, she was strapped down and begging.

"No, sorry," he said. "And the name is Ren."

"That's what I said," she said, looking mad and really too cute. She shoved a mass of auburn curls over her shoulder.

He gave her an indulgent smile. "Okay, just stay indoors for the rest of the night and I won't have to arrest you."

"You sure you couldn't use a shot, Chief?" Julia said, holding up a half-empty bottle of tequila.

He shifted his gaze to her. "I'm sure, but you should stay here tonight, to be on the safe side."

"I planned to. Even brought my jammies."

He shifted his gazed back to Grace, who was smiling at him again. "You two should call it a night so you can hopefully survive."

Grace straightened, threw her shoulders back, thrust her magnificent breasts out, and saluted him, almost falling over again in the process.

"Yes, sir, Chief." She dropped her hand. "You sure you don't want to do a shot?" she asked. Before he could answer, she asked Julia what she thought of him.

"He's really cute," she said between giggles. "A little too authoritarian for me, though. I like men who can be managed."

Grace gave Ren her back and had her fists on her hips again. "Gabriel can not be managed," she said indignantly.

"I wasn't talking about him."

"That's who you want. Don't you agree, Ren?"

Since he had no idea what they were talking about, he remained silent, thinking that was his best option.

Before Grace could question him again, Julia said, "No, he has some chick baking him cookies and bringing them to his apartment."

"Does not," Grace insisted.

Julia looked down into the shot glass. "Talked to him last night, and she was over there, ringing his doorbell. How rude is that?" She directed this question to him.

"Pretty rude?" he asked, hoping it was the right answer.

"Damn straight. I mean, really," she said in a disgusted tone, rolling her eyes. Then she smiled, and turned to Grace. "He sure is hot. Can we keep him?"

"No, he'd have to sleep with me," she said giggling. "Or Sam."

He looked at the adorable woman in front of him. She was cute when she let her hair down, figuratively and literally and *cute* was not his type. Even if since he'd met her, he'd done nothing but fantasize about the woman, and what positions he would like to have her in. With that ass, he would dearly love to have her up on her knees, her butt in the air...

And the other problem was the feeling sliding through his system. Something that wasn't lust, something he was just too uncomfortable to analyze. But somewhere in the back of his mind, he knew that there'd be no way of fighting it. Still, he stomped it back, far back into the corner of his mind and decided to ignore it. Grace turned to face him with a drunken, sloppy smile.

"Oh," Julia said, in a surprisingly sober tone. "I'm sure he wouldn't mind that." Ren looked at those green eyes that warned him to be careful.

"You're silly," Grace said, facing Julia and giggling again. "He doesn't want to sleep with Sam."

Julia took the shot of tequila she'd been holding onto during the conversation. She let out a bark of laughter, spraying the liquor all over Grace, which caused Grace to fall back onto the ottoman, laughing so hard she had to wipe away tears. Ren decided to make his escape before he did something really stupid. Like throw the woman over his shoulder, carry her across the street, and fuck her until she couldn't see straight.

"Well, ladies, I'm going to go do some more unpacking, so I'll leave you to your tequila."

"I'll walk you to the door," Grace said, jumping up so fast off the ottoman that she almost fell over again. She followed him to the door, which put them just out of sight of the living room.

"Thanks again for getting rid of Darian," she said.

"Maybe you should file charges, get a restraining order."

"Naw, I can handle him. If not, I have a big, strong, virile lawman living across the street," she said, her eyes twinkling.

He opened the door and as he turned to say goodnight, she kissed him lightly on the cheek.

"What was that for?"

"It was a kiss," she said, smiling. "You know, to thank you."

"Ah, Grace," he said, his voice taking on a husky edge as he ignored the warning signals that were going off in his head. "That's not a kiss."

Ren slid his arm around her waist, drawing her closer, watching her eyes first widen in surprise and then dilate with arousal. He'd told himself to steer clear, avoid anything resembling a relationship with Grace. All thoughts of avoiding her disappeared as he bent, and touched his lips to hers. They were soft and cool and wet. He nibbled on her lower lip, keeping his eyes open, staring into hers. Passion clouded her golden, whiskey depths. They fluttered shut. She opened her mouth with a moan, and he took complete possession.

His tongue intruded past her lips. He could taste the lime and tequila she'd been drinking, along with a hint of salt. He shifted his grip, bringing her fully against his body, making sure there was no way she could mistake just how hard he was. Her soft, heated sex pressed against his cock. She entwined her arms around his neck, and spread her fingers through his hair. He almost lost all control when her tongue reached into his mouth. Tentatively, then more boldly, it danced with his.

His hands moved from her waist, and tangled in her magnificent mass of hair. His fingers slipped through her silky curls, every fiber of his being concentrated on her. Her lips. Her body. Her scent. Lust spiraled through him. One hand began moving back down and grabbed the hem of her shirt.

Reality intruded when a car honked in the distance.

With a groan of regret, he set her away from him and said, in a voice hoarse with unspent passion, "Now *that* is a kiss. Lock the door." He kissed her forehead, and then walked out the door, shutting it behind him.

"Oh, my," he heard Grace say through the wood.

He hadn't been this frustrated since high school, but he smiled as he heard another "oh, my" from Grace. He walked down the steps, and across the street to do some more unpacking. He'd probably be up half the night anyway.

ഗ്രൂ

Julia awoke with her head pounding. Every time she tried to open an eyelid, bright sun scalded her vision and the room spun. She decided she would be better off just staying passed out on Grace's living room floor. Only the pounding wouldn't go away. Someone kept taking a sledgehammer to her brain.

Then Sam barked, and she realized that someone—who was about to die—was banging on the front door and ringing the doorbell. Slowly, she sat up. "Alright, already!" she yelled, regretting it immediately. Her head spun like a carousel. Her stomach flip-flopped. She got up on her hands and knees, taking deep breaths.

Bit by bit, she crawled to the front door, wondering where the hell Grace was. Grabbing the knob, she pulled herself off the floor. The pounding had finally stopped by the time she yanked open the door to find Grace's brother, Gabriel, standing on the front porch, looking as good as ever. His worried expression quickly changed to one of confusion.

"Julia?" he asked.

"No," she said sarcastically as she gingerly walked to the kitchen. Her back ached from spending the night on the floor while her head pounded from the tequila. "I'm your fairy godmother."

Oh, she smelled coffee. Thank God Grace was a planner. And to hell with the devil for placing Gabriel Michaels on

Grace's front porch when she looked and, she thought, taking a whiff, smelled her worst.

"What are you doing here?" he asked. "It looks like a tornado hit this place."

"Grace and I did tequila last night."

She grabbed a coffee cup and poured the rich mocha into the mug, stifling a yawn. One day, fifty years from now, she might think this was funny. Right now it struck her as the way her life usually went. Throughout the many years she had known the Michaels family, Gabriel had repeatedly seen her in the worst light.

He was the one who was home the night she'd returned from her disastrous first date with Jimmy Callander. It had also been her last date with the creep. She'd made the mistake of parking with him, a decision she regretted to that day. There were still times she thought it *had* been her fault for leading him on, just as he'd said. But apparently Jimmy didn't understand that no meant no, and unfortunately, at that point in her life, she hadn't had the strength to fight the bastard off. He'd clamped his hand over her mouth and forced himself on her. Then the jackass had the nerve to dump her six blocks from Grace's house. She'd walked the whole way, clothes rumpled and torn, her hair a mess and her make-up smudged with tears. Gabriel had been the only one to see her like that, and he hadn't said a word. He's just looked at her with a dark, disapproving glare that had shamed her to her soul. It'd shaken her so badly, it had taken her weeks to tell Grace about the incident. Grace, on the other hand, had been so incensed that she'd stolen into the locker room and put itch bombs in Jimmy's underwear. Jimmy had been in so much pain he had to stand on the sidelines of the game the next night because it was too uncomfortable to sit.

It didn't matter what Gabriel thought anyway. He liked his women petite, with bleached blonde hair and big boobs. Three things the opposite of her.

"So you seemed to have finished up your revisions," she stated with skepticism in her voice. "It's a good thing I was here last night. The Triple D was bothering Grace again." Julia was satisfied to see the protective gleam in his eyes. If there was one redeeming quality Gabriel had, it was his love for his sister.

Gabriel fought to control the rage.

"He was here? At her house?" he asked. He had only met the bastard three times in his life, and he really didn't know anything about him. All he knew is that he had hurt Grace. That was enough for Gabriel to see red. "What did he do?"

"Not much," Julia said, smiling wryly. "Grace told him to go play with himself. Then that lawman from across the street showed up and took care of everything."

"What lawman?"

"The one who rented your parents' house. I guess he witnessed Triple D bugging us so he came over and scared him off."

"Well," Gabriel said, refocusing on Julia. "At least she wasn't by herself. The real question is, why is he here and why he's bugging her?" He paused and took in Julia's appearance. "When did you cut off all of your hair?"

"September," she replied. "It was so humid and I couldn't take it anymore."

"Well, it's really short," he remarked, thinking that it brought out those dark green eyes of hers and emphasized the killer cheek bones. For a moment, he regretted she'd cut it he'd had some fantasies about seeing it spread against the pillows around her head while he made love to her, or spilled across his lap while she went down on him. But now, seeing all those angles and shapes in her face, plus the exposed neck, gave him a whole other set of fantasies.

"I didn't know my folks rented out the place," he said, shaking his head to stop thinking about things that were never going to happen. "I'd planned on crashing there. Sam doesn't like sharing a bed."

"Tell me about it," she said with a snort. "I slept on the floor. Did you get everything done you needed to with your book?"

"Yeah," he said distractedly, trying to think of another place to stay.

He loved his sister, but that mutt of hers drove him crazy. Bad enough the damn thing didn't give an inch when it came to the extra bed, but he was loud as hell and had a nasty habit of drooling in his shoes and pissing on his suitcase. *No, thank you*, he thought.

The problem was, most of his old friends had either moved or were married, with children. Not many wives would be happy to put up with an old friend crashing on their couch, even if he did have a book on the *New York Times* list.

"Well, crap. That means that I'm going to be on the couch." He looked over at Julia, who closed her eyes, enjoying a sip of coffee. "I guess you don't have any extra room over at your place?"

Her eyes flew open and she choked. "Well, I do have a guest room," she said, avoiding eye contact. "But I'm not so sure that you would like it. You know, you need your space. At least, I think that writers need their space. Anyway, you could hardly keep an eye on Grace from my place. It's over on the other side of town." That argument rang false since driving from one side of Cannon to the other usually took less than five minutes.

"Well, you did mention this chief seems to be keeping an eye on her," he said.

He mentally chastised himself because he knew staying at Julia's would drive him crazy. Still, anything was better than Sam.

Julia poured herself a little more coffee. Although he knew she was uncomfortable with the conversation, her movements were as economically graceful as always. He could sit and watch the woman for hours. No matter what she was doing, she always reminded him of a dancer. Her long slender fingers and competent hands moved through a series of movements that seemed to be orchestrated.

What bothered him the most was that she seemed to have something at her house that she wanted to protect or hide. "You wouldn't mind if I crash for a few days, would you? We could work together to help Grace. I promise not to get in the way."

"Yeah," she said and then averted her eyes. "I guess I could spare some room if you stay out of my stuff."

"Like what, Julia?" he asked, taking a step forward, causing her to back up against the counter.

"Just stuff," she said, her voice had raised almost an octave. "And I am really particular about my personal space." Her hair was sticking up on one side of her head, there were mascara marks under her eyes, and she was still the most beautiful woman he'd ever seen. That ivory skin against those red bud lips made his mouth water and his cock stand at attention.

"As long as you promise to stay out of my office, then okay," she said, adding quickly: "But just for a few days."

The doorbell rang, sending Sam, who'd retreated upstairs in his room, into a frenzy of barking.

Julia closed her eyes, and muttered an unintelligible curse. Gabriel went to the door, hoping it was Darian. He really wanted to take a piece out of the guy. Instead, he found a rather large, dark-haired man standing on the porch. His brown eyes took in every detail as he studied him, and Gabriel knew there wasn't much you could hide from this man.

ജ്ഞ

"I'm looking for Grace and Julia," Ren said. "Just thought I'd check up on them after witnessing their...uh, conditions last night."

Jesus, every time he came over here there seemed to be a man present. What did Grace do? Keep a supply of them in her storage shed? He took in the hazel eyes, and reddish brown hair and realized this must be the brother.

"I'm Ren Morello. You must be Gabriel. I'm a big fan of your books."

"The chief?" Gabriel asked, opening the screen door. "I just got in this morning. Nice to meet you."

Ren followed him to the kitchen, where he saw Julia leaning against the counter. She really was a mess.

"How you doing this morning, Goulia?"

Her lips curved. "Just fine, Len. I take it you met Gabriel?"

"Yep. How's Grace doing this morning?"

"Grace is doing just fine," Grace said, her husky voice drifting through the kitchen. "But she's really wondering what the hell everyone is doing here."

Ren turned and looked over his shoulder. His mouth lost all moisture. She wore an old football jersey that covered her to mid thigh. Her hair was piled in a lose ponytail on top of her head, with a few streamers of her red curls escaping and trailing to her shoulders. Every hormone in his body bounced to life, and any blood in his brain headed south.

"Gabriel? What are you doing here?" she asked, catapulting toward him.

Her brother opened his arms, and enclosed her in a bear hug. "Just finished up my latest revisions, and decided to stop by and see my favorite sister." With that said, he picked her up off of the floor and gave her a loud smacking kiss on her cheek.

"I'm your only sister, butthead," she said, walking over and filling a cup with hot coffee. "Anyone else?"

"Nope," Gabriel said.

She turned her questioning eyes toward Ren.

"No, thanks," he said. "I need to get to the office and get a little work done. I just wanted to make sure that you two were all right."

"I'll walk you to the door," she offered, brushing past him.

"It's just a few feet, Grace. I think Ren is a big boy and can handle it himself," Gabriel said, earning him a cold look from both Grace and Julia.

ॐ

"You know," Julia said to Gabriel after Ren and Grace left. "I think we need to set some ground rules."

"Like what?" he asked suspiciously.

"You leave Grace and her lawman alone. I think he's attracted to her and your sister needs to have a little fling."

"Something I'm sure you know all about, Julia," he said, disgust evident in his voice.

She wanted to tell him to go to hell. She wanted to scream that borderline date rape on one occasion didn't make her a slut, but it would do no good. Instead she took a steadying breath.

"First of all, you have no room to talk, seeing as how you have such *friendly* neighbors where you live." She was glad to see the smugness fade from his eyes. "And, second of all, she needs a little fun. Her last real relationship was with Darian. That was almost six years ago. She needs someone else to balance out that disaster. And third," she said, making sure he was looking her in the eyes. "No guest room for you, buster. You'll be sleeping with Sam if you aren't careful."

ℰℭℛ

"Thanks for coming over here and checking up on us," Grace said. "We don't do this on a usual basis, but every now and then, we need a break. You know, gotta let off some steam."

She followed Ren out onto her porch. It probably wasn't the smartest move because Mrs. Garvey stood in her front yard, watering the same flower for the longest time while she tried to listen to their conversation. If she kept it up, she was going to kill that flower.

"Yeah," he said. "I can imagine all the pressure you're under. Every time I come to your house, I run into a man."

"Not any that count as competition," she said, smiling. "I'm going to have to rethink my whole sexual history after that kiss last night."

"Yeah, uh," he said, looking uncomfortable for the first time since she had met him. "Grace, look, I'm not the kind of guy..."

79

"Ren," she said, amusement intermingling with exasperation in her voice. "I'm only kidding. I know that you were only trying to prove a point last night."

But it would sure be nice for it to have been for another reason altogether. Like he found her body irresistible, and he'd been overcome with lust. She almost snorted out loud at that thought. Men like Ren didn't go for short, dowdy, bookish college professors. They went for women like Julia.

Good Lord! She hoped that wasn't the reason he had come over that morning. Julia would never date him. Julia never dated anyone. But it would still hurt to know that he was attracted to Julia and not her.

"Look," Ren said when he noticed a little panic creep into her eyes. "It wasn't only that. I find you really attractive."

She snickered. *Yeah, right.*

"But you're not the type of woman for me," he continued.

Of course not, she thought.

"I'm not heavily into commitment," he said. "You strike me as the type who would require a lot of attention and then expect something more than sex. I'm not saying there is anything wrong that. Just that I am not ready to jump into that mess again, at least anytime in the near future."

The whole time Ren stood there, telling her he wasn't interested in a relationship, scenes of slipping that T-shirt over her head, and exploring what lay beneath with his hands and mouth flashed through his mind.

"So," Grace said slowly, as if talking to a three year old, snapping him out of his reverie. "You're saying if I was another type of woman, you would not think twice about sleeping with me?"

"I think I made that pretty clear last night." He crossed his arms over his chest to keep his hands from reaching out, and grabbing the one lose tendril that had escaped the loose ponytail. Every sexual instinct told him to touch her, to pull her to him. His logical instinct screamed denials.

"So, if I were to say I'd be happy to have an affair, no strings attached, you would be interested?"

Grace was as likely to say such a thing as she was to sprout wings out of her lovely, lush ass and take off flying across the yard. Ren had come in contact with too many women like her, especially since his divorce. They all assumed that just he'd been married once, he was ready to do it again. That somewhere along the line, he'd be trained. Why women thought being divorced proved that you were good marriage material was beyond him. They were *wives in training,* none of them satisfied until they had you moved in, pre-nupped and a ring on their finger. He took a deep breath and looked her straight in the eye. "Yes. If you were the kind of woman who would accept that agreement, I would, without a doubt, be very, very interested."

She leaned toward him, placing a hand on his chest. He could smell fresh soap and shampoo on her. His stomach clenched. Uneasiness invaded him when he saw the seductive smile.

"Ren?" she asked, licking her lips as if anticipating a forbidden treat.

Instantly rock hard, he wondered why the zipper on his jeans didn't explode from the sudden pressure from his cock.

"Yeah, Grace?" he asked in a hoarse whisper.

"I'm interested in an affair, no strings attached."

Chapter Seven

The blood drained so fast from Ren's brain, he feared he'd faint. "No, no you don't," he sputtered. "You want the house and the kids. You aren't the type of woman who jumps from bed to bed."

He backed away from Grace. Pure panic rose and tightened his throat. It was okay to fantasize about the woman, but there was absolutely no way he was going to give in to the urge.

"How do you know what kind of woman I am?" Grace asked.

"I just know. You don't want a guy like me—who can't be tied down."

"I don't know about that. You did mention handcuffs last night."

He backed up, bumping into the railing that ran around her porch. Keeping his eyes on her, he slowly walked to the stairs. She started toward him, but he held up his hand. "You stay away from me. You're trouble with a capital T, woman."

He reached the bottom of the stairs, and turned to walk down the path. Grace's husky laughter followed him, mocking him.

"Coward!" she yelled after him, laughing again.

"You're damn right!" he yelled back, without turning around. He jogged across the street to his truck.

℘℺

Grace woke late and grumpy Monday morning. Though she'd argued against her schedule this semester, Dr. Peterson had overruled her, stating she was the youngest, newly tenured, and the only one that actually wouldn't pass out without a good ten hours of sleep. She really loved working with all the professors in her department, but sometimes being the only one under the age of fifty was a little too much to bear.

After rushing through a cup of coffee and banana for breakfast, she hurriedly dressed, cursing the fact she'd forgotten she was out of stockings. She tugged on her pantyhose, slapped on a dress, then slipped on her most comfortable pumps, and headed out the door.

She pulled into a staff parking space, thinking one of the few reasons teaching an eight o'clock class was great was the parking. A cold front had blown through the area the night before, bringing a chill in the wind as it whipped through her curls. Waking up late had prevented her from pulling her hair back. By the end of the day it was sure to be a mess.

When she reached her office, she hesitated after unlocking her door. Her lights were on, which was odd because she never left them that way. Even between classes, she turned the lights off to keep the room cooler because the vent in her office didn't work well.

She shut the door and walked to her desk. Dropping her briefcase on the floor, she plopped down in the chair, relaxing for a couple minutes before she had to hike over to class. An electric hum filled the silence of her office, and she turned to find her computer on, her *American Monuments* screen saver playing on the monitor. She knew before she'd left Friday afternoon she'd turned her computer off.

She moved the mouse around, clearing the screen and found someone had been in her files. Her documents folders were all open on the computer desktop like someone had searched through their contents one by one. Uneasiness settled in her stomach.

It's nothing, she told herself. The cleaning crew must have hit the button somehow and turned it on. Yeah. Then bumped my mouse a couple of times vacuuming under my desk, and opened my desktop icons. Or maybe Dr. Gump had come into my office to borrow something as he did sometimes.

She reached to grab the tests she'd graded and found they'd been rifled through. A chill crept down her spine but she squashed it. She knew she was overreacting. *So they knocked over my papers, too,* she thought. *They must have picked them up and stuffed them all together on top of my desk again. Just an accident.*

But accident or not, she definitely was going to talk to Peterson about this after her eight o'clock. No, first she would check with Dr. Gump, make sure he hadn't accidentally hit something when he'd been in her office, then she would talk to Dr. Peterson. She scooped up the tests and her notebook, and headed out to the lecture hall that was halfway across campus. She made sure to shut and lock her door.

As she hurried down that sidewalk in front of the history building, she realized if she half-ran, half-walked, she'd make it just five minutes late.

"Grace!" an annoyingly familiar voice yelled behind her. "Grace, wait up!"

She quickened her steps, to no avail, because Darian was taller than she was, his legs eating up more ground.

"Grace, really," he said, grabbing her arm. "I've been yelling at you forever." He halted her by jerking her arm back. His fingers dug into her skin through her coat.

"I have a class that started five minutes ago, Darian, and I'm not really in the mood to deal with you again this morning." She yanked her arm free, and set off to class again.

"Grace, I thought maybe we could do lunch."

"I teach the next two hours, have some grading and advising time for the next two after that, and then lunch with Gabriel. Really, really busy, Darian. I don't have any time for you."

"Well," he said. Irritation sounded in his voice. "I guess I'll try to catch you later."

"Sure," she said, without turning around.

If she could find a way, she really needed to check to see if there was any mental illness in Darian's family.

ಐಗ

Julia couldn't believe she was in such a situation. Here, in her house, her private sanctuary, sat Gabriel, bigger than life, at her breakfast bar in her kitchen. He'd invaded her home.

She wasn't a small woman, but Gabriel was a few inches taller than she, all muscle and brawn, dwarfing her kitchen. She'd barely slept last night, thinking of him down the hall from her. The only other person who'd spent the night in her house was Grace. Her father hadn't stepped a foot inside the city limits of Cannon in the past few years let alone her house.

Julia's father usually refused to make the trip and summoned her to Dallas to complain about whatever she had done wrong.

This was different. Other than the occasional repairman or cable guy, there had never been a man in her house before. Especially overnight.

And especially not this man. His auburn hair was a shade or two darker than Grace's, the tips burnished by the sun, bringing out the green in his hazel eyes. Gabriel wasn't built like Ren Morello, who reminded Julia of a linebacker for the Dallas Cowboys. Gabriel had muscles, but there was a lean, streamlined quality to his build. His face showed little sign of age, except the laugh lines around his gorgeous eyes. Every time she looked into those eyes, a shiver of warmth crept into her stomach and slid lower. Every beat of her heart sent a pulse of heat to her sex.

"So, Jules, what do you think about Grace's new guy, Ren?" he asked.

"I think he's great."

"Yeah, well, I was just wondering if he was right for Grace. He seemed kind of unrefined."

Julia let out a sharp, loud laugh. "Yeah, right. She had refined. He was an asshole. Ren is nice and he checked up on her. Grace needs someone male to check up on her. Someone not related by blood."

"I don't know. He's too good looking for her."

Before she could think, her hand whipped through the air and connected with the side of his head.

"You asshole! How dare you say that? Your sister is gorgeous. It's just that kind of attitude that makes her off limits to the jackasses in this town." She smacked him once more.

"Ow, dammit, Julia, quit smacking me," he said, grabbing her wrist. "I just meant she wasn't used to it. I'm afraid a guy like Morello knows the score. Grace doesn't. She's thirty-three. I know she's not a virgin," he said with a wince that made her smile. "But she is still an innocent."

Julia pulled her hand free, trying to ignore the warmth where he'd encircled her wrist. "My instincts say that he's a good guy. And another thing in his favor is he hated Darian on sight."

"Okay, okay. He seemed like a good guy. But Grace isn't like me and you, Julia."

She stared at him.

"We both know the score. Grace always looks for the best in people. You and I both know that sometimes the best in people isn't all that good."

Pain flashed in her chest, and she turned away.

"Yeah, I agree." She poured herself a cup of coffee. "I have some work to do." At that, she walked down that hall to her office and shut the door.

ဢလ

"Why are you staying with Julia instead of me, Gabriel?" Grace asked.

They were at The Old Wagon Wheel Restaurant waiting for the lunch. Gabriel and Grace had spent many a family dinner there. The outside of the restaurant looked like an old saloon, with a huge wagon wheel out front, hence the name. The large interior was filled with wooden booths. Each sported salt and pepper shakers made from old beer bottles, a roll of paper towels, and a Coke glass filled with silverware.

If you were lucky enough to sit at one of the booths against the wall, your table came equipped with your own individual miniature jukebox. The only problem was they hadn't changed the assortment of songs since the Michaels started coming there twenty years earlier. At the moment, Gabriel studied the selection intently, hoping Grace would let the subject go. Grace settled back on the uncomfortable booth seat, crossed her arms, and awaited his answer.

"You know, Grace, that mutt of yours drives me insane," he said finally. "Besides, you don't have an extra. Sleeping on the couch doesn't appeal to me."

"But Gabriel, Julia doesn't let anyone spend the night," she said. She was about to continue, but Delilah Cantrell brought their lunch.

She set their plates in front of them, then leaned forward to let Gabriel see her fabulous cleavage, and asked, "Is there anything else you need?"

Delilah was one of the many former high school cheerleaders Gabriel had dated. She was a year older and divorced with two kids, but still had a great figure. She'd pulled her heavily highlighted blonde hair into a ponytail on top of her head. She had sky-blue eyes, full rounded hips, and very full—and undoubtedly expensive—breasts.

"Thanks, Delilah, but I think we're fine," he said, smiling.

"Why, you remember my name!" Delilah exclaimed, all wide-eyed and giggling. "That's so sweet of you. And here, I heard you ran off and published this big, best-selling novel and made all of this money off it. I figured you forget about all of—"

"Of course he remembers you, Delilah," Grace said, cutting in. Gabriel could tell she was getting disgusted with all the adoration. "You lived down the street from us. Hell, he dated you for a while. That was before you decided to dump him for Denny."

Gabriel watched Delilah's baby blues spark with annoyance before she masked them with sensuality once more.

"Well, let me know if you need anything," she said, purring this toward him and pointedly turning her back on Grace. He watched her sashay toward the kitchen, ignoring other customers with equal and deliberate ease.

"That is really disgusting," Grace said.

He was surprised that, for once, he agreed with his sister. Usually he would have taken Delilah up on the offer she flashed him with that killer body. He remembered she'd been insatiable when they had dated in high school. And, from her demeanor, he could tell she hadn't changed one bit. But, for some reason, the seductive voice and promise of sexual satisfaction he saw in her eyes struck him as slimy.

He poured ketchup on his fries. "Yeah, but I'm thinking she'll make a great murderer for my next book."

She smiled then dug into her meal. They ate in comfortable silence for a few minutes, but Gabriel knew Grace was not going to let the subject of where he was residing go.

"Like I was saying before your adoring *fan* interrupted us, Julia usually doesn't let anyone stay over," she said, pausing to pop a fry into her mouth. She munched on it for a few seconds. "I don't think that her father has even seen her house. He hasn't been back for years. They had a huge fight."

"What would they have to fight about?" he asked, perplexed. He knew that after Julia's mother had died at the end of her and Grace's junior year in high school, Mr. Jacobs had left Cannon. Julia had lived with them that last year of school. He assumed that during the few years she'd spent in Dallas after that, she had lived with her father.

"*This* time, it was her wedding," Grace said.

"Wedding?" Gabriel asked a little more sharply than he intended. He mentally warned himself to calm down. "I didn't know she was seeing anyone seriously." He tried to sound casual and failed.

"Well, Julia really hasn't...that is to say she isn't involved with anyone. Her father had someone hand-picked from his corporation. Some senior VP."

"And they fought because...?" Getting information from Grace was proving to be an aggravating exercise. She finished off her cheeseburger, wiped her mouth, and looked him in the eye. It was then that he knew she'd been baiting him.

"She refused. She told him anyone who worked for him was sure to be some kind of yes-man." She paused to take a sip of tea. "He banished her from Dallas, which made her happy. Or so she says."

"I didn't know they had so many problems."

"Oh, they don't have problems. Julia said to have a problem in a relationship, they'd have to *have* one."

"So, is that why she has such superficial flings?" he asked.

He looked up when she didn't answer, and swallowed a curse at the anger in her eyes. Shit, she was pissed. Tangling with Grace when she was mad could leave some serious scars. And there was no one outside of her family, Grace protected more than Julia.

"Answer me this," she said in a clipped voice. Yep, she was really ticked. "When was the last time you saw Julia with anyone?"

"Well, mmm..."

"What amazes me is that you—the king of the one night stands with big-boobed bimbos—has the nerve to judge anyone.

I would think after all these years you would know Julia." She grabbed her purse. "Tell me, Gabriel, if she was such a loose woman, how is it that you never scored with her?"

"I never tried," he said in an angry but quiet tone. A few heads had turned when Grace raised her voice. He was sure that this scene would be replayed in detail all over town by sundown. "I was afraid I wouldn't stack up to the competition." Great, now he was pissed, too.

"Really, I love you Gabriel, but sometimes you're thickheaded," Grace said. "I think you hold onto that idea of Julia being promiscuous so you have a reason to stay away."

She stood up beside their booth, dropped her purse on the table and angrily shoved her arms into her coat.

"You would be amazed what you would find if you would just look beneath the surface." She scooped up her purse and stormed out, leaving him with the bill and an uneasy feeling.

ଚ୍ଚର

A couple of weeks later, Grace decided to call it an early day after her morning lectures and head home for a little research. Mrs. Garvey, her next-door neighbor, had called and left a message that Sam was out of the house. How the dog had escaped was beyond Grace, but she hurried home as fast as she could.

The first thing she noticed as she pulled into her driveway was Sam sitting on her front porch. She knew Gabriel was going to stop by, but his car wasn't around and he'd never leave Sam outside. Worry crawled through her and bunched in her stomach. She rubbed it, trying to ease the panic that was almost choking her.

Sam bounded off the porch as soon as she opened her car door. He skidded to a stop before her and barked, then turned, ran to the house and stood barking at the window in her office. Grace noticed the screen was lying on the ground and hurried over. Her window was wide open, her curtains billowing in the breeze. Alarm slinked down her spine.

"Sam, let's head on over to Mrs. Garvey's."

Sam trotted behind Grace as she walked across the lawn. Her next-door neighbor, widowed ten years earlier, kept everyone up to date on the happenings of the street. Grace had found out she and Ren had been the subject of many debates that took place on front porches, sidewalks, and at backyard cookouts since the morning she had propositioned him. Before she reached the front porch, Mrs. Garvey was coming through the front door.

"I told you he was out. Wouldn't let me take him into the backyard," she said, giving Sam an affectionate pat. "He just kept coming up to me and barking. Then he would run to the front of your house."

"I really appreciate you calling. Did you see anyone around my house today?" Grace asked.

"No, sure didn't."

Grace tried to control her rebellious mane. Her hands trembled. She dropped them to her sides. She would *not* fall apart like some ninny head.

"Any idea how he got out?" Mrs. Garvey asked.

"It seems someone broke into my house. The window in my office is wide open and the screen is lying on the ground," Grace said, trying to keep her voice calm. Mrs. Garvey's eyes had widened at the announcement, and Grace really didn't want to alarm her. "I was wondering if I could use your phone. I left my cell at the office. If someone was in my house, I don't want to disturb anything."

Grace could see the alarmist in Mrs. Garvey was doing battle with the busy body. It scared her someone might have broken in her next-door neighbor's house, but Grace was sure she'd dine out on the story for weeks.

"Sure thing," she said, hurrying up the stairs and opening her screen door for Grace. "You know where the phone is."

ℰℛℛ

Ren had just hauled a couple of truant kids out of the arcade and dragged them into his office when the phone rang. Mrs. Janey answered, and Ren ignored the conversation until he heard Grace's name mentioned. He abandoned the boys and stalked over to her desk. She hung up the phone and smiled up at Ren. Today, her lipstick was orange, and her hair was a lime green.

"Was Barney outside?" she asked him.

"No, I sent him out to Jed Vickers' place to check out some vandalism. Why?" he asked casually.

Ms. Janey rifled through the mess on top of her desk. "Well, according to Grace Michaels, someone broke into her house."

Chapter Eight

Ren's gut clenched. He fought to control his reaction and said, "I'll take the call." He ignored Ms. Janey's raised eyebrow. "And get on the horn to their mothers." He gestured towards the two boys. One of the boys visibly paled, and both of them swallowed nervously. Apparently being hauled in by the Chief of Police didn't frighten them as much as this new and horrific prospect.

Ren grabbed his keys and sunglasses, and headed out the door, trying to stamp down the fear that had reared its head as soon as he'd heard Grace's name.

Within five minutes, Ren pulled up to the curb in front of Grace's house. She stood next to a petite gray-headed lady dressed in a moo-moo. He recognized Mrs. Garvey as the head busybody on a street of busybodies. She had her arm around Grace's shoulders.

Grace turned as soon as she heard his truck. She wasn't crying, but her shoulders sagged with relief as he got out of the vehicle and headed toward her.

"Ren," she said. "I didn't expect you." He had done his best to avoid her the past two weeks since she'd proposed a no-strings-attached relationship. For two people who lived across the street from each other, they'd done no more than wave.

"Yeah, well, I was there when the call came in," he said. "What happened?"

She told him what had happened. "I went to Mrs. Garvey's house and called," she said as they walked together toward her house. "I thought it would be best not to touch anything."

They reached the porch and Ren touched her arm. "Sam was okay?" he asked and then continued when she nodded. "You stay here while I go in and check out the situation."

Grace's front door was locked, so she gave Ren her keys. He unlocked the door and went in, his gun ready. The first thing he noticed was the window in her kitchen was open. There was a trail of mud from the kitchen window, through the kitchen, and down the hall to Grace's office. Careful not to touch anything and avoid the mud smears, he walked down the hall and peered into the office.

Mud was everywhere. It was tracked from the doorway to the desk. The hum of her PC filled the room. He followed another trail from the desk to the loveseat in front of the window. The quilt on the loveseat was smeared with mud. After checking the entire first floor, he slowly crept up the stairs. First he peeked in at what he figured was the guest room and then her room and bathroom. Retracing his steps, he joined Grace on her lawn.

Mrs. Garvey was gone, probably doing her duty to alert the neighborhood. Grace was bent at the waist, hugging Sam, making cooing noises, thanking him for protecting her house. She straightened when she saw Ren, and Sam gave him a friendly bark.

"I'm going to call it in and have Barney do some fingerprinting. There's mud everywhere, but the only place disturbed is your office."

She frowned causing a little crinkle in between her eyebrows to appear and she bit her lip. "Was anything taken or damaged?"

"Other than the screen," he said and motioned toward the window. "And all the mud, it doesn't look like it. If I didn't know better..." His voice faded.

"What?"

"It looked like someone had been looking for information or some particular item. Your desk had been rifled through and your computer was on."

Her eyes widened slightly at the comment. "That's strange. You know..." The crease returned between her eyebrows. "Something like that happened a couple of weeks ago at my office at the school."

Surprise came first; then aggravation. "Why the hell didn't you say anything? You should have told me about it."

"I forgot about it. Nothing was taken. Besides, I wouldn't contact you about that anyway. It would be the campus police who would investigate, right?"

He was pissed again. He really didn't know why, but he was.

"I wasn't talking about that," he said through clenched teeth, barely controlling his raging temper. "I was talking about the fact I'm your *friend*, and you could have told me."

"Oh." She sounded surprised. "I never thought to tell anyone. Really, Ren, I didn't even remember to tell Julia or Gabriel."

"Well," he said, mollified and a little embarrassed by his reaction. "What was similar?"

"Someone left my computer on. They had gone through my desk and tried to get into my files. Now that I think about it, all the lights were on, too. I never leave my lights on, especially on a Friday. I figured it must have been the cleaning people, but I really didn't think much about it, because I was rushed that day. I'm sure if something had been stolen or damaged I would have remembered."

"Okay." He reached into his jacket and pulled out his cell phone. "Let me call Barney and get a fingerprint kit down here. As soon as that's done, I'll need you to go through the house and see if anything is missing."

Before he could call him, a siren sounded, going full blast. Barney sped down the street, swerving to miss a few park cars. He ended up with one of his tires on Grace's curb when his cruiser came to a stop. He jumped out of the car, pulling his oversized hat onto his golden curls, and slammed the door. He raced toward Ren, excitement bubbling from him.

Ren placed his hands on his hips and sighed.

ଓଗ

A couple of hours later, Grace walked through her house with Ren. She had deposited Sam next door with Mrs. Garvey, and given him a huge rawhide bone for his bravery.

Ren had been right. Her lace curtains lay on the floor and were covered with mud, as was the windowsill. There were smudges of mud on the counters. With each step she took through the rooms, her composure cracked a little. The only thing holding her together was the warm comfort of having Ren by her side. For some reason, his mean expression and silent support kept her from crying.

"This is actually the worst of the mud," Ren said, interrupting her thoughts. "There's some tracked in through the hallway and on some of the rugs in your office, but for the most part this is the worst of it."

She turned to find him giving her an encouraging smile tinged with a little anxiety. Smiling to reassure him and herself, she said, "Don't worry, Ren, I won't fall apart on you."

If the rest of the house was where most the mud was, the office was where most of her belongings had been moved. She heard the computer as soon as she entered. "I never leave it on," she said, nodding in the direction of the monitor. "Dr. Campos from the math department had lightening strike his house last spring semester and it fried his computer. I've always turned it off ever since."

"Anything else?" Ren asked.

"Well, of course the window, and the mud on my quilt and sofa," she said, trying to calm down when she heard the hitch in her voice. She blinked rapidly when tears gathered in her eyes. Some butthead had gotten mud on her grandmother's wedding-ring quilt. She took a deep breath. "Other than that, there doesn't seem to be anything missing." Thinking to get her quilt, she took a step in direction of the window, but Ren laid a hand on her arm, stopping her.

"You need to wait until Julia can get here to help you, okay?"

She took another deep breath and nodded. He led the way out the house and when they stepped out onto the porch, Julia and Gabriel pulled up in the little red convertible. Julia rushed forward, anxiety etching her features, but Gabriel was another story. He looked as furious. Both fists were clenched at his sides.

"Grace," Julia said, hugging her. "We came as soon as we got your message. I'm sorry it took so long. Gabe was out and I was working. I tried to call your cell, but I just got your voice mail."

Grace hugged her back, and the gesture warmed her. Julia hardly ever displayed any kind of affection. Every now and then, something would overwhelm her, and the emotions she hid so well boiled over.

Grace looked over Julia's shoulder, and saw Gabriel with his fists still clenched, ready to do battle for her. She squeezed Julia once more and released her, knowing he was ready to explode. He encircled her with his arms. She allowed the warmth to seep from him, and relaxed for the first time since she had gotten the call about Sam.

"How you doing, dork?" he asked, his voice still edgy with the draining anger.

"I'm fine, loser," she replied, managing a feeble smile. "Someone broke into my house, flung mud all over the place, then rifled through my office. Luckily, Sam chased them back out the front window." She stopped to take a shaky breath and then smiled again. "I thank God nothing happened to Sam."

He returned the smile. "I'm buying that nuisance a side of beef." He shifted his golden-green gaze to Ren. "I take it you're going to catch the bastard who did this." It was a statement, not a question.

Without looking at Grace, Ren said, "This is not the first time this has happened. Someone did the same thing to her office a couple of weeks ago."

He held up his hand when Gabriel looked like he would explode right there on her front lawn. "I just found out about it," he said pointing in her direction. "She didn't to tell anyone."

"Hey, I forgot," Grace said. "I swear. It was that day we went to the Wagon Wheel for lunch. You remember, we had that argument. Plus, I was a little distracted that day."

Yeah, by an ex-fiance, by being late for work, and by thoughts of one very sexy, totally uninterested law officer. Especially the law officer. Every night she fell asleep thinking of Ren, what it would feel like with his hands on her. Then she would awake, hot and sweaty with her hand on her sex and the memory of a dream of which he'd been the star. A girl could only handle so much.

She motioned toward her house. "Nothing like this happened. The computer was left on, but nothing much else was disturbed."

"What did you two fight about?" Julia asked.

"That's not important," Gabriel said quickly. "The real question is why didn't Grace tell us anything?"

"I forgot about it," she said through clenched teeth.

"Don't worry, I plan to investigate the first break-in, too," Ren said.

"It didn't look like this," Grace said. "Someone got in with a key or they picked the lock. There weren't any signs they forced their way into my office. Maybe that was why I didn't think anything about it."

"You need to think about what's in your office, especially your computer, worth getting," Ren told her. "Something someone might go after here if they couldn't find it at the school."

She thought about tests she kept, but they were all on disk. *My research maybe? But who would be after...*

The thought trailed off as the answer came to her. *Darian!*

"You thought of someone."

"Well..." she said, stalling, wanting to talk to Julia about it first.

Ren looked her in the eyes. "Don't even try to lie, Grace."

"How long have you two known each other?" Gabriel asked, laughing.

"Two weeks," he said, without looking away from Grace.

She tried one last tactic. "But he hasn't talked to me since I propositioned him."

He took hold of each of her upper arms and shook her, just enough to get her attention. "Don't even think you can get me to change the subject. Who are you protecting?"

"I'm not protecting anyone." He shook her again. "Darian. He might be interested in my research."

Ren dropped his hands and shook his head. "Why would you protect that jackass?"

"I'm not," she said. "But I didn't want to say anything and cause any problems for anyone." She saw anger leap in his eyes. "I really don't care if anything happens to him, but I couldn't bear to accuse someone who was innocent. No matter how much of a jerk he is." She looked up to her house. "Look, as much as I'd like to stand here and argue about this some more, I really want to get my house cleaned up. Okay? Then, I'll be happy to discuss it with you."

"Okay," he said, grudgingly. "But we will get into it tonight." The steel in his voice convinced her he was very serious.

ℴℴ

It took a couple of hours to clean up the mess and get Sam settled back into the house. For thirty minutes after he came home, Sam ran through the kitchen, hallway, and office, sniffing every crevice, and barking at the window every few minutes.

Since she'd planned on grocery shopping that afternoon, Grace didn't have enough to feed them. She absolutely refused to leave Sam alone. That gave them a choice of chicken, burgers or pizza. They voted for pizza, and Julia and Grace thought it best to send the men instead of having them pacing the confines of the house.

"Grace," Julia said as she stood on Grace's front porch watching Gabriel and Ren drive away in Ren's truck. "You know it was Dawson."

"No, I don't."

Julia turned and looked at Grace and said, "Yes, you do. Who else would be looking for your research?"

Grace smiled wearily because she knew Julia was right on target. "Well, yeah, and I know Darian has done this before when he stole some research from me when we were both at UT." He had nearly ruined Grace, in fact, and broken her heart, too. But she didn't want to think about that, because truthfully, the pain hadn't lasted overly long and now she was mostly embarrassed at having been so naive. "He also doesn't like to work for anything," she said. "That's why he screwed Ronnie. He made her do the work. In more ways than one."

Julia snorted at that. "It would be the only thing that would make sense. He's after that research on Cord McPherson. I bet on it."

Grace sighed and walked back into her house. Although she knew Julia was probably correct in her assumptions, for some reason she really didn't think Darian would do something that evasive. Although, thinking back to the scene with him and Ronnie, she started having second thoughts. And thirds. Okay, she was pretty sure it was him, but just wanted to be positive. She didn't want to falsely accuse anyone, even that dickhead.

Making a mistake like that could lose her the trust of Dr. Peterson and the other professors.

She bent and patted Sam on his back as she passed him on her way to the kitchen. Julia followed her, and they both sat at her dinette table.

"What I can't understand is why he would do it again, and with such bad planning," Julia said, thinking out loud.

"I'm not sure it was totally his idea last time." She noticed Julia was getting set to argue with her. "I think Ronnie had a lot to do with it." She shrugged. "Darian isn't the smartest man in the world."

ഇ൚ര

After gorging themselves on pizza, all four of them settled in Grace's living room. Grace sat next to Julia on her sofa while Ren plopped down in the oversized chair. Gabriel sat on the floor on a big red pillow and leaned up against the sofa next to Grace's legs. She really thought he was overreacting. All through dinner, he kept touching her as if to reassure himself she was okay. He even went so far as to suggest they call their parents. She nipped that in the bud. She shuddered at the thought of their RV parked in front of her house.

"So," Ren said, pulling her attention back to him. "I want you to explain why you think it may be Dawson."

"Then Ren and I are going to go and kick the shit out of him." This came from Gabriel. She could see he was getting all riled up again.

"I will only explain if Gabriel promises not to do anything," Grace said. Gabriel hesitated and then finally he nodded. "Okay, I met Darian my first year of teaching at UT."

"We already know that," Gabriel said.

Julia leaned forward and conked him on the head. "Shut up so she can finish."

"We sort of gravitated toward each other because we were the only two new professors that year. Anyway, we started dating and eventually moved in together. Then, around December, I found an old official border map from Mexico that could have made my career. Not only did it show the agreement with the Spanish government had the border much further north, it had the documentation from the Texas government agreeing to the border. I knew this one document would make my dreams of getting published a reality and really establish me in the field. It would have opened up a whole world of academic opportunities for me.

"Before I told anyone what I'd found, I confided in Darian," she said, taking a breath. Remembering all the pain and bitterness, she was surprised to find they both had faded over time. "He seemed thrilled, but I knew there was something bugging him. Well, to make a long story short, he stole all of my research. He got the book published, and then received the one tenure track position UT had at the end of the year. We had both been hired as adjunct professors. I couldn't prove anything. Dr. Peterson called, told me they had a tenure track professorship here, and encouraged me to apply. The rest, as they say, is history. No pun intended. That's why I thought of Darian."

Everyone was quiet for a second and then Grace sighed. "But I could be wrong, and anyway, it doesn't matter. He may have had access to my office, but none of this is going to do him any good. I keep everything protected by passwords."

"Okay," Ren said. "So other than Golden Boy, are there any other people who could get into your office?"

"No. No one who would steal research, and break into my home."

"Okay, I'll check out what Golden Boy was doing this afternoon," Ren said. "Barney is questioning the neighbors. Maybe by tomorrow we can come up with something." He glanced at both Julia and Gabriel. "In the meantime, I think you need someone to spend the night."

Grace felt a little tingly zing of excitement. She would be more than happy to make room for her own personal bodyguard. "I know the logistics of moving Sam would be a nightmare," Ren continued. "He seems determined to protect the home front. So Gabriel or Julia should spend the night with you." The zing plummeted. "Just to be on the safe side."

"I'll stay," Julia said. "Gabriel can't fit on the sofa."

"Yeah, right," Gabriel said with a snort. "I'll stay. Sam will probably sleep with Grace anyway." Julia looked like she would argue, but relented.

After saying goodnight to both Ren and Julia, Gabriel and Grace headed back into the kitchen to clean up. As they headed up the stairs, Grace in the lead, Gabriel asked, "So, Grace, did you really proposition the Chief?"

She didn't turn around. "It really isn't any of your business," she said wearily. "Do you think Julia will be okay alone?"

"Grace, your house was broken into, not hers."

They had reached the top and Grace headed to her room. "You left some things when you were here last time. I put them in the dresser." She opened her bedroom door to find Sam stretched out on top of her bed. *Looks like Ren was right.*

Gabriel turned and headed to Sam's bedroom. "Well, I'm going to head to bed," he said. "See you in the morning."

"Thanks, Gabriel," Grace said. "You know I love you."

He turned, closed the space between them and gave her a hug. "I know. Ditto from me."

ॐ

Grace awoke sweating. She couldn't breath and an incredible weight pressed down on her chest. She opened her mouth to take a breath, and sucked in a mouthful of hair.

"Sam," she said, muffled by his torso. "Get off me." She took both of her hands and pushed the dog away.

Slowly she stood up and grabbed her favorite pair of pajama bottoms. The dog had made a furnace for a bedmate, and she had worn only a tank top and panties to bed. She was sure, she thought with a small grin, Gabriel would not want to see her walk down the stairs dressed like that.

The aroma of coffee reached her. Gabriel had to be awake, because she'd been too distracted to set it up like she usually did every evening. She heard Gabriel's gravelly voice, intermixed with a higher, southern-accented voice and knew Julia had made it over to her house early. She smiled to herself, knowing that Julia was not big on mornings.

When she walked into the kitchen, Julia sat at the table, looking outside. Wearing a ball cap and sweat suit, she looked so different than the polished, sophisticated woman she showed the world. Her arms were crossed beneath her breasts and she was breathing heavily. Grace glanced across the kitchen. Gabriel leaned up against the counter by the sink, glowering at Julia.

"Before you tell me about it, I need caffeine," Grace said, causing them both to jump.

She walked over to the coffee pot and found her favorite mug already waiting for her. She poured herself a cup, doctored it up with a dollop of cream, sat down opposite of Julia, and sighed.

"Okay, I'm ready. What was the argument about this time?"

Julia drew in a shaky breath and said, "I wanted to spend the night tonight. There's a complication at my house. Gabriel needs to find another place to crash. I know I don't want to be at my place, and there's not enough room for all of us here."

"The reason for that is...?" Grace asked.

Her voice on the edge of hysteria, Julia said, "It happened. He's in my house and he won't leave." Grace studied Julia for a moment. She knew only one person could send her into this hysterical state.

"Your father," Grace said.

Julia nodded. "He says he won't leave until we talk."

Chapter Nine

"My father was sitting on my front porch last night when I got home," Julia said.

"Why is Walter here?" Grace asked. She took hold of Julia's fisted hand and tugged until Julia looked away from the window. "What does he want?"

"Maybe he just wanted to spend time with his only child?" Gabriel suggested, earning him a cold stare from Julia.

"No, he wants something else." She turned to look out the window, closing her hand into a fist again. Grace knew she was trying to calm herself down. "He just showed up. Acted like it was no big deal. Like he always shows up out of the blue to visit. I'm not spending any more time than I have to with His Highness."

"Well," Grace said, trying to think of something to calm Julia down. "Maybe he's not staying long. Maybe just a couple of days."

"He said he had something to discuss. I'm sure it's the same crap he wanted to discuss this past summer."

"Okay, first things first," Grace. "You can stay here, Julia." Grace looked over at Gabriel, sensing he was going to argue the point. "Before you say anything, don't worry. You can stay, too. I have a blow-up mattress in the attic you can bring down, and we'll work out some kind of sleeping arrangements later. I know it's not the best but it will have to do. I have classes all day, and tonight, too, and Sam is still pretty on edge about what happened yesterday. Having you guys here would be nice, and if you were here alone, Gabriel, he'd drive you nuts." She looked over at the clock. "I need to get ready to go. You two duke it out over the details, if you want."

She gulped down the rest of her coffee, and left the kitchen.

ఴᦓ

Julia didn't feel like duking out anything with Gabriel, however. She followed Grace down the hall to her room, sat on the edge of Grace's unmade bed and watched her get ready for work. The initial panic wedged into her stomach had lessened, though anxiety still threatened to consume her. When she realized she was biting her thumbnail, she immediately took it out of her mouth and mentally chastised herself for resorting to her teenage habit.

"What am I going to do, Grace?" she asked. "He says he's not leaving until we have that talk. Gabriel was bad enough, but what am I going to do about Walter?"

Grace still thought it was weird that Julia called her father by his given name. Julia had started calling him *Walter* when she was thirteen and he missed her dance recital for the fifth year in a row. She quit dance and never called him *Daddy* again. She said a real father would have been there. Grace knew she was right, but it was still weird.

"Did you talk to him this morning?" Grace asked as she leaned closer to the mirror to apply a little eye makeup. Silence filled the room. "Julia, honey, you have to face him at some point. Knowing him, he'll just come here to find you."

"Yeah, well, I was afraid when he first showed up that he'd found out about my writing. Walter would not be happy to learn that his daughter was actually Genevieve Dubois. Can you imagine?" Like Gabriel, Julia had needed a creative outlet and she found that in writing, not to mention a lucrative income. But, unlike Gabriel who wrote hard-edged thrillers, Julia wrote erotic thrillers with a bit of romance, and they'd become some of Grace's favorite books.

"He would probably worry about getting kicked out of the Petroleum Club if anyone found out," Julia said, frowning. "No, I was a coward this morning. There has been too much going on and I didn't want to deal with it. I'll face him, but on my own time. I just needed a break."

Grace chose a brown tweed pantsuit to wear. As she dressed, she considered why Walter would show up. "You don't think there could be anything wrong with him, do you?"

"Other than the fact he's as faithful as an alley cat? No. Why, what could be wrong with him?"

Grace considered how best to approach the subject and decided the direct approach was the best. "You don't think he could be sick, do you?"

"Walter, my father, who runs every day? The vegetarian? Probably not. People like him live forever. All that cold hate seems to be some kind health food. I'm not sure which it is, but either he is here about me getting married, or he's found out that I'm Genevieve Dubois and has come to kill me to put me out of my misery."

&)Q

Gabriel stood in the hallway outside Grace's bedroom, not meaning to eavesdrop, but unable to help it. There was no way—positively no way—that Julia could be Genevieve Dubois. The thrillers Dubois wrote were international best-sellers. Her latest had knocked his own off the *New York Times* top ten. They were skilled stories of obsession and control, and highly erotic, or so he had been told. He'd never read any of them. Dark, dangerous and decidedly naughty prose wasn't his style. But come to think of it, it *was* Julia's. Especially since he'd read more than one reviewer remark on her sarcastic humor.

He stood in the hallway, and tried to wrap his mind around the idea. He heard footsteps moving toward the door, and headed to the guest room.

Their voices finally faded down the stairs, and he breathed a sigh of relief. He sat down on his bed, and thought about Julia and Genevieve Dubois. It occurred to him that when he had stolen a peek in her library, which was in her off-limits office, he had see all of the Genevieve Dubois books.

Could she really be a best-selling author? What if Julia and he shared more than love for his family? Disbelief, irritation, and curiosity tumbled through him. He would have to do a little investigation, and filter out the truth from the fiction. Then, he and Little Miss Julia would sit down have a talk about being truthful.

ಬಿಂಕ

Ren sat at his desk with the door to his office closed, going over the information Barney had gathered. He was damned impressed with his deputy. Despite his age and inexperience, his report was more thorough than what a lot of veteran policemen would have provided. Fingerprints had been lifted off of the windowsill, the kitchen counter, and all over the office. On top of that, Dr. Dawson had been seen in the area. No one had actually seen him go into or come out of her house. But Ren had a gut feeling Darian had something to do with it.

When he had seen Grace this morning, she'd given him a brilliant smile and a friendly wave, then got in her car and left. She didn't seem any worse for the episode. He'd been tempted to offer his protective services last night, but from the look in her brother's eyes, Ren had known he wasn't needed. Relief had intermingled with regret but it was better that way. Protecting Grace would lead to things he knew would cause both of them to regret. Like waking up in bed with one shapely, warm woman.

He hoped he wouldn't have to arrest Gabriel for kicking the shit out of Dawson. Hell, Ren himself had been so furious about Grace's story last night, and what he knew about Dawson's cheating, he'd wanted to kick his ass.

The thing that surprised him was the sheer amount of possessiveness that had gripped him. Whenever he thought about Grace and what the bastard had done to her, Ren wanted to turn back time and shield her from the hurt.

A knock sounded at the door. "Thought I would drop by and see what Barney dug up on the jackass," Gabriel said, sticking his head through.

"So you've already decided that Dawson's guilty," Ren said, knowing he agreed with Gabriel. It was getting harder and harder to draw the line between his job and his personal life. It was just another reason that he could not act on any attraction. He had to run a clean investigation so he could nail the asshole.

"Yeah and so have you," Gabriel replied. "You know there's no one else who would need to break into her house and her office." He paced in front of Ren's desk. "Hell, I'm ready to beat the shit out of him just for the crap he pulled six years ago."

Ren eyed him for a second. "I'll have to arrest you if you go after him without provocation."

Gabriel stopped pacing, and faced Ren. Barely restrained anger rolled off of him.

"I saw the look on your face last night," Ren warned. "Don't step over the line. Grace would kill me if I had to book you. Besides, I wouldn't want to deal with all the press arresting a major celebrity would cause."

"Well, if you don't want to discuss that, how about we discuss the fact that my sister propositioned you?" Gabriel asked, with a protective gleam in his eyes.

"Hey, I told her no way. I told her I'm only into no attachment. She said she didn't care. Your sister is a real sweetheart, but really, she's not my type."

An angry flush colored Gabriel's cheeks. "She not attractive enough for you?" he asked.

Ren could only stare at him. If Grace had been another kind of woman, Ren would not hesitate feasting on every succulent curve. Like every other time he thought about Grace, he felt the same familiar coil of lust sink down into his belly. He still couldn't believe a conservative, slightly dowdy history professor could make him drool, but it was just not possible for him to ignore that body. *And her hair,* he thought. *And well, that seductive smile on those full lips when she jokes with me. All I want to do is grab all those silken curls and pull her body up against me...*

Ren wondered whether or not Gabriel knew he wanted to make a meal out of his sister. He could gorge himself on all that golden flesh for weeks. How could her brother not understand that? Okay, so brothers may not look at their sisters as a meal.

"No, I find her very attractive," he said, and Gabriel's eyes narrowed. "But your sister is the kind of woman who is

113

conservative. You know, the type who settles for one guy at a time, for a house and kids. Not for me, Michaels. I tried once and sucked at it. So, although I find your sister extremely attractive, I'm not even thinking about being anymore than friends with her."

"Okay," Gabriel said. "I trust you." He was quiet for a second or two. "Did she really proposition you?"

"I swear she did. That first morning you were here. I've tried avoiding her ever since. Your sister may have picked up a drinking problem at some point, because that seemed way out of character for her."

Gabriel snorted. "Well, she's usually not so self-assertive with men, but she never thinks before she acts. That's why Julia and Grace have always gotten into so much trouble. Julia would come up with the crazy ideas, Grace would encourage her, and then she'd be the one ending up injured usually. Their senior year they calmed down a bit. Julia moved in with us so most of their disasters happened in the kitchen when they were cooking. Well, there was that one bra-burning incident that caused a lot of smoke damage to the bathroom."

Ren raised one eyebrow in question.

"They'd been studying the women's movement. It was the November of their senior year. Dad was so pissed."

"Why did Julia move in her senior year?" Ren asked.

"Her mother died and her father moved to Dallas. She wanted to finish high school here, so she moved in with us. I figured the reckless behavior took a dive because of her mother's death and living with my father." Gabriel smiled. "You can't get much by my old man."

"Her father moved, just like that?" Ren asked.

"Yeah, about two weeks after the funeral. That's Walter. It was no love match between her parents. It might've been at one point, but all I ever saw was bitterness. Walter already spent most of his time in Dallas anyway. He's been married three times since." Gabriel said, sitting down in the old leather chair opposite Ren's desk. "He's in town now, by the way. I don't think he has been back since he left."

"He didn't make her graduation?"

"No. Anyway, to get back on the subject of that dickhead, Dawson—when are you going to question him?"

"I'll probably stop by the college today. If I can't catch him there, I'll have to go by his house." Ren stood, grabbing his keys and sunglasses. "And don't even think I'm going to let you come with me to intimidate him."

"I gotta do something," Gabriel protested. "Julia has taken over Grace's house to avoid her father, and I really don't want to go over there. Let me help you out. I could talk to a few people. Might pick up on something about Golden Boy. Folks will say things to me they would never say to you." Ren raised an eyebrow and waited for an explanation. "You're the Chief of Police, and you're an outsider. If they say something to you, it makes them look like a tattler, but if they say something to me, they're just talking about what's going on. It worked wonders when I was a journalist."

Ren thought it over for a moment. Gabriel could be helpful with a different perspective. And, although he had yet to meet anyone who liked Dawson, people were more likely to talk to someone they knew well before they'd talk to the police. It might help in gathering more evidence against him.

"Okay, but no fighting with him," Ren said. "I mean it, Michaels. Not only would I have to put you in jail, but your sister and Julia would be furious."

He walked through his doorway and out into the office. Gabriel followed behind him. "Ms. Janey, I'm going over to the college," Ren said, looking her in the eye as he added: "Don't call me on the radio. It doesn't work and I have my cell. Do we understand each other?"

She pursed her lips. "I like using the radio."

"Ms. Janey, it doesn't work. If there's an emergency, you need to use the phone. It's more reliable."

"Okay." She released a disappointed sigh. "I really like using the radio. Using the telephone is so boring."

"Use the cell," he said, putting on his uniform hat. "Michaels, you coming?"

They drove to the Murray History building on campus. "I'm going to talk to Peterson and I want you to handle the secretary," Ren said as they headed for the faculty offices.

"Got it," Gabriel replied with a nod.

Ren opened the door and found an older, rather petite woman sitting behind a huge mahogany desk. He placed her age somewhere in her early fifties, but could've been wrong. Her head was covered with salt-and-pepper curls. She had bright brown eyes and the most beautiful coffee-colored skin he had ever seen. She wore half glasses, perched low on her nose while she studied a document she held in her hands. She looked up when they entered and smiled.

"Well, Gabe, honey, how are you doing?" she asked in a musical southern voice that reminded Ren of all the Southern Belles he'd met in Atlanta. "Grace said you were in town. It took you long enough to make it in to see me." She stood, and came around the desk. She barely reached Gabriel's shoulder, and he was an inch or two shorter than Ren. He hugged the secretary and released her.

"How has been Stan been doing in Houston?" he asked.

Her face broke into an even more beautiful smile. "Stan is doing fine. The practice is going well and Sheila and he are going to be giving me another grandchild by next spring. Now, I take it this is the young man who all the ladies are drooling over."

"Ren, I would like to introduce you to Ms. Cecilia Bennet, the real brains behind this department. Cecilia, this is Ren Morello, the new police chief."

She smiled again. "Nice to meet you. You might just beat this lady killer here," she said, giving Gabriel's hand a squeeze. "I'm assuming you're here to talk about the break-ins?"

"So you know about the one here too?" Ren said. Cecilia walked around her desk, and sat in her massive burgundy leather chair. She motioned for both of them to sit.

"Yes. Grace told me about it this morning. I let her know she should have told someone about it. I hate to say this, because I'll sound like some idiot on the news, but this really is a safe town, as I'm sure you know. The campus is usually so safe, I don't worry about being here late by myself."

"Do you often stay late?"

"No, usually just at the start of the semester, when we're trying to get everything going." She lifted papers off of her desk. "Well, and when that Dr. Gump gives me his things to copy."

"Is Dr. Peterson in?" Ren asked. "I need to talk to him about the break-in here."

"Sure thing," she said. She picked up the phone, and dialed the extension. Within a couple minutes he was seated in front of Grace's boss, and Gabriel was off to the copy room with Cecilia.

After about fifteen minutes, Ren was ready to strangle Dr. Peterson. Not only was getting information out of him hard, but the man also had been the one to brag to several professors

117

down in Austin about Grace's discovery of Suzanna Cannon's diary. If the assumption that Dawson was in town to steal research was right, Peterson had been the cause of all of her problems. The professor, of course, was oblivious that it might have been his fault.

Ren thanked him and headed off into the department to see who else he could talk to. Cecilia was still not back from the copy room, so he strolled out the door and came face to face with a short, heavy man with glasses and graying hair. Bright blue eyes peered out from behind the thick lenses and he smiled.

"You must be the new lawman in town," the man said in a thick German accent. "I am Dr. Homer Gump." He stuck out a pudgy hand and Ren accepted the shake. "I am to understand Dr. Daniel is to be arrested for breaking and entering, yes, yes."

"Dr. Gump, I'm not sure what you have heard, but we are still investigating," Ren said.

A door opened down the hall and a gaggle of students poured out of the classroom. Dr. Gump motioned for him to follow. Ren walked down the hallway, trying not to smile at the professor's waddle. Even so, the man moved surprisingly fast for his girth. He walked through an open doorway that led to his office. Each side was filled with bookshelves. From the ceiling to the floor, the shelves were stuffed full. A large oak desk sat at the opposite end of the room. Behind it was a large window, covered in blinds. A credenza covered in mementos and pictures sat beneath the window.

Gump waddled to the chair behind the desk, and motioned for Ren to take a seat. "Now, Chief, what are you going to do about this idiot bothering our Grace?"

"*Our* Grace?" Ren asked.

"Well, Fredrick and I think of her as our own niece. She looks after us. I know you would not know this by looking at me," Dr. Gump said, leaning forward as his chair squeaked. "But I happen to be very forgetful when it comes to anything outside of my studies." Ren decided not to mention he noticed the socks that didn't match, and the line of shaving cream on his chin. "Anyway, I told Grace I do not like this Dr. Daniel Dawson. He is shifty. Little beady eyes." Gump leaned back and the chair squeaked again. "Besides, anyone not smart enough to hold onto Grace has to be an idi*ot*," he declared.

Before Ren could comment on that, there was a knock at the door. Grace's little face peeked through the small rectangular window. Her eyes widened when she recognized Ren.

"Come," Gump said, with a smile that belied it had been a command. Ren could see that the affection was returned when Grace opened the door, and came in. She held a stack of papers in her hand, and placed them on Dr. Gump's desk. The warm smile she gave the professor slithered down Ren's spine. He wished she would give him a smile like that. Every time he saw it, he wanted to slide his hand inside her frumpy suit and cup her breast, feel her nipple pebble as he rubbed his thumb...

"Ren, what are you doing here?"

"I found him in the hallway and wanted to tell him my theories about the dirty, lying Dr. Dawson," Gump said. Grace walked over to stand beside Ren, her scent growing stronger as she neared. His palms itched to grab hold of her and kiss her. He mentally cursed his reaction. Confusing the investigation would not be smart.

"I told you he was dirty," Dr. Gump said, his little blue eyes serious and determined.

"Dr. Gump, you really shouldn't make assumptions like that." She admonished him as if he were five years old and telling a fib. She crossed her arms beneath her breasts, emphasizing what had been hidden underneath another ugly tweed suit.

"Doctor, did you happen to see him here at the office on the third of the month? That was a Sunday?" Ren asked. He was anxious to get going. Grace's earthy scent filled the office, and sent his senses spiraling.

"No. Fredrick and I stayed home. Didn't even go to the library, as I recall."

"Fredrick?" he asked, noting he had said the name twice in less than five minutes.

"Dr. Meyers and Dr. Gump share a house together," Grace said. She turned towards the rotund professor. "You were busy that weekend with tomatoes, remember?"

Gump looked confused for a minute, then his face brightened with recognition. "Of course! You came by on Saturday to talk to us about your research and your upcoming celebration with Julia."

Ren decided that he had spent enough time talking to the professor. He stood, about to thank Dr. Gump, when a screech echoed in the hallway. He rushed out the door and found Gabriel standing over Dawson, fists clenched. A tall, rather emaciated bottle-blonde was kneeling at Dawson's side, hovering over him, as if to protect him. Her bright pink miniskirt had hiked up a few inches and Ren could see the tops of her stockings. The black sweater she wore was two sizes too small, and the neckline plunged halfway to her navel.

"Michaels!" Ren shouted, rushing forward.

The blonde had moved over to pull Dawson's head onto her lap. The professor had a bloody nose and his head rolled from side to side.

"I told you not to mess with him," Ren said to Gabriel, weary and irritable. "Now I have to arrest you, damn it."

"I don't care," Gabriel replied, rubbing his knuckles. "It was worth it."

"Gabriel, what the hell are you doing?" Grace asked as she shoved her way through the crowd of students that had gathered. She was about to admonish him more, but Ren saw that the blonde caught her eye and Grace paled. "Hello, Ronnie," she said.

"Hello, Grace," the woman, Ronnie said, sarcasm diminishing any welcome. "I should have known this was your brother, with all that red hair."

At that point, there was a groan from Dawson. His eyes flickered and opened. "What...?"

"Don't worry, darling," Ronnie said, patting his cheek, but her eyes were on Ren, and they traveled from his head to his feet. "There's a lawman here and he'll set everything straight." She helped Dawson to his feet, and brushed off his jacket.

"Morello," Dawson said with a sneer. "I want to press charges against this man. He came out of nowhere and attacked me for no reason."

"I had a reason, dickhead," Gabriel shot back. "You broke into Grace's house and office."

"I did not!" Dawson yelled, his voice taking on a slight whine. "That's slander."

"Since I'm here, why don't you tell me where you were yesterday afternoon?" Ren asked.

"Why, I was at home—then and the day they say someone broke into her office."

"Really?" Ren asked. "Then a couple of her neighbors must have been mistaken. They claim they saw you leaving the scene of the crime yesterday."

"They must have been," Ronnie drawled. She had plastered her body next to Dawson, but gave Ren a look, as calculating as it was cold. "He was there with me, both the Sunday of the office break-in and yesterday. We spent most of the day making love." She looked at Grace with a smirk. "We were really busy. Couldn't be disturbed." Ren chanced a look over at Grace and was surprised to see her cheek dimple with a smile.

"Unfortunately, I know from experience that would hardly take more than ten minutes, Ronnie," she said. "You'll have to account for more time than that."

ഇൻൾ

As she opened the door to the library stairwell, Grace replayed the scene from that morning in her head. Gabriel had been arrested, booked and released to a very upset Julia. She had assured Grace she would keep an eye on him for the rest of the day. From the gleam in Julia's eyes, Grace was sure he had been chastised for acting like an idiot. She was still worried about the situation with Julia's father, but Grace realized there wasn't much she could do. Actually, she thought, if they were to fight it out, they would be better off. They may never talk to each other again, but what would that hurt? It seemed to do more damage the more time they spent together.

She'd returned to finish up her classes for the day and do a little research on the Cannon family at the library. A few stairs from the bottom, someone from behind whispered her name.

She began to turn, but before she could, a hand pressed into her back and pushed. Grace lost her balance, her feet coming out from underneath her. Helpless to stop, she fell face first down the last few steps, hitting with a thud.

The side of her face slammed onto the concrete floor, her cheek and forehead banging sharply. Blinking, she tried to force the stars twirling in front of her eyes to disappear. She heard the click of high heels, and then nothing at all as darkness pulled her down.

Chapter Ten

Ren sat in the outer office and looked at all the information they'd gathered, silently cursing. Even if they could shatter Dawson's alibi, it would be hard to get him fingerprinted. They just didn't have enough—not even circumstantial evidence—to get an arrest warrant.

He leaned back in his chair, pinching the bridge of his nose with his forefinger and thumb, and closed his eyes. He'd planned on picking up Grace tonight after her last class, but she had said she needed to do a little research and could drive herself home. He was about to head out to see if she made it home okay when the phone on Ms. Janey's desk rang. Being the only one on duty, he hurried over to answer it.

"Cannon Police Department, Ren Morello."

"Oh, thank the Lord. This is Zach Nelson, sir," said the young anxious voice on the other end of the line. "I didn't know who else to call."

"What seems to be the problem?"

"We had a little accident out here at the college. One of our professors took a tumble down the library stairs."

Immediately, uneasiness curled Ren's stomach. "Who's the professor?"

"It's Grace Michaels." The thought of her hurt sent a shiver of dread curling through him. "She came around once, but she's unconscious now. I called the local clinic and they're sending the paramedics over, but I figured we needed some other kind of authority for this sort of thing."

Icy fingers of fear slithered around his spine and froze his brain. He couldn't think, couldn't contemplate her being hurt.

"Authority?"

"I'm sorry. I'm one of the campus police. When she came to, Dr. Michaels claimed someone pushed her. That was before she passed out again."

"I'm on my way," Ren said. "You need to get into her files and call her home number." There was no way he could remember her number, not with his heart pounding and his brain short-circuiting in panic. He'd be lucky if he could remember how to drive. "Her brother is her next of kin, and he's staying over there tonight." He slammed down the phone, and grabbed his hat and coat as he headed out the door.

It took Ren about five minutes to make it to the campus. Cannon's only ambulance sat out front of the history building with its lights still flashing. He ran up the steps, burst through the door and found a group of onlookers surrounding the paramedics. They had put Grace on a gurney, and his breath caught in his chest when he saw a bloody gash on her forehead.

With each step, Ren reminded himself that head wounds bled profusely. *It's worse than it looks,* he told himself. *It's worse than it looks.* As he approached, he noticed a rather attractive looking older woman holding Grace's hand and softly saying her name. A female paramedic leaned over her, dabbing at the wound. He knelt beside Grace and relief flowed through him when her eyes fluttered.

ഇൻ

Grace was having a horrible dream. She felt as if someone had knocked her over the head with an unabridged dictionary and then decided to pour salt into the wound. She heard a woman saying her name, but every time she tried to open her eyes, light scalded them, and she shut them, unable to deal with the pain. Then she heard Ren say her name. She opened her eyes, but closed them immediately, trying to block out the painful light. She moaned and tried to lift her hand, but found that someone had hold of it.

"That's right, honey," Ren whispered, close enough to her ear, his warm breath caressed her skin. "Open your eyes."

She fought the pain and tried. Worry etched Ren's face as he leaned over her. She wondered where she was, and why she was in so much pain.

Then, in one blinding instant, the hand at her back and her helplessness as she fell rushed to the forefront of her mind. She tried to block out the memories by closing her eyes, and going back to sleep.

"Grace," Ren almost shouted. "No, no, honey. You have to stay awake."

She opened her eyes and Ren smiled, albeit strained. She tried to return it with one of her own, but pain radiated from her cheek.

"Grace," Lorna Patterson said softly in her south Texas accent. Lorna was always so protective towards her. Grace knew she must be worried. She really was the one of the sweetest women she ever knew. "How are you doing?" Grace tried to turn her head to look in her direction, but someone held onto her head.

"No, Grace. You need to hold your head steady." She glanced up to see Michelle Hubbard smiling down at her. Once again she tried to smile, but the sting in her left cheek stopped her. "Yeah, you're going to be hurting a little from that bruise."

"Someone pushed me." She tried to sound forceful, but it came out in a whisper. "I felt a hand on my back..."

A cell phone rang. Ren's voice was measured and calm as he spoke. While talking on the phone, he kept hold of Grace's hand, stroking her knuckles with his thumb. For some reason, each time that callused thumb stroked, she felt reassured.

From his end of the conversation, Grace realized he was speaking to Gabriel. He told him to meet him at the clinic. Hanging up the phone, he leaned over Grace again.

"I'm going to follow you in my truck, okay?" he said.

"Sure," she said in a whisper again. "Was that Gabriel?"

"Yes, and he has his hands full with Julia, who's hysterical. They're going to meet us at the clinic. She wanted to come here, but we should be on our way by then."

Ren breathed a sigh of relief when she smiled. It was a crooked one-sided smile, because he was sure the bruise that was already turning purple on her left cheek hindered her facial movements. But the muscles in his stomach relaxed a bit. The paramedic had bandaged her head. The line of freckles that marched across her nose stood out against the paleness of her face.

"I'll see you as soon as they pull in," he said, saying it to reassure himself more than her.

"It's a date," she joked. The paramedics pulled the gurney up, and wheeled her out into the ambulance.

Even though they had the siren on, Ren was sure it took a lifetime to get to the clinic. When they pulled up, he saw Gabriel and Julia standing just inside the entrance. Julia started forward, as if to rush the ambulance, but Gabriel stopped her by putting his arm across her shoulders and whispering in her ear. She nodded but looked out the entrance with concern clouding her eyes.

Ren got out of his truck and watched the paramedics pull Grace's stretcher from of the ambulance. He raised his hand and plowed it through his hair, noticing he was shaking. He didn't believe he'd ever been so scared in all his life. Not even his rookie year, when he'd faced down a kid with a gun, hyped up on PCP. This was much worse. Because this time, other than investigate, he could do nothing but wait to see what the doctor said.

He followed Grace and the paramedics through the entrance, and walked to where Gabriel and Julia sat.

"What the hell happened?" she asked in an accusing tone.

"Jules," Gabriel gently. "Let Ren tell us what he knows." She seemed to calm down, but still eyed him suspiciously.

"She was pushed down the stairs," Ren said. "She said she felt a hand on her back, and someone shove her. That's all I have right now. It doesn't look like she has any broken bones, but she might have a concussion."

"It was probably the jackass," Gabriel said in a tone so calm that anyone listening would think he was rational. But his eyes told a different story. Anger turned them a darker shade of hazel, and murder brimmed in them. "Dawson didn't learn his lesson today."

Julia turned, knocked his arm off of her shoulder, and said, "You idiot. You aren't going after him again. You've already been arrested once today." Ren watched in fascination as

Gabriel shoved his hands into his pockets and looked sheepish. Julia shook her head and sighed. "Darian would never do anything like this."

"I thought you didn't like the man," Ren said. She rolled her eyes and faced him. He now understood why Gabriel shut up. He had never seen a woman so mad.

"Of course I don't like the jackass. But I know what he is."

"And what, pray tell is that?" asked Gabriel. She glanced in his direction and then turned back to Ren.

"He's a coward. He's a lazy, stinking, two-timing coward. He'd rather sneak behind someone's back than face them. Knowing the Triple D, he's at home with an ice pack on his nose and that slut on his lap, rubbing his ego to make it feel better."

Her voice hitched on the last sentence. And Ren, who had a very manly fear of tears, decided he would change the subject, when the doors leading to the examining rooms opened.

A doctor walked toward them with a serious expression on his face. "I'm Doctor Edwards," he said with a nod toward Ren. He apparently wasn't a stranger to the family because he greeted Gabriel and Julia by name. "Wish I were seeing the two of you under more pleasant circumstances," he told them, pressing Julia's hand momentarily between his own. "Well, Grace definitely took a bad blow to the head when she fell down those stairs, but other than a few bumps, bruises and scratches, she should be fine. The gash on her head looks worse than it actually is, but I did put a couple of stitches in it. Thankfully, she doesn't seem to have a concussion, so she should be able to go home tonight. Someone should stay with her, and she should stay home tomorrow. You two can go on back to see her."

Edwards smiled encouragingly as Gabriel and Julia walked side-by-side back to her room. "Now, I take it you are the Ren she mentioned at least fifty times in the last few minutes?" he asked with one raised eyebrow. Ren nodded and the doctor continued. "She told me she wanted you to take her home, and she kept insisting she was pushed."

"What do you think?" he asked. If the day of Ren's introduction to Grace was any good indication, she wasn't the most graceful or least accident-prone women in the world. But somehow, Ren knew this wasn't just a case of clumsiness, no matter how characteristic.

"Well, she's had a bit of a fright, and she's still shaken up from it." The doctor looked toward the room. "But there's no way to tell what happened, not from her injuries. The important thing is that it could have been worse. A lot worse."

I know, Ren thought.

"You can go on back while they finish up her paperwork," the doctor said. "I'll have the nurse go over some instructions for you before you leave."

Ren thanked the doctor again and headed back to Grace's room. He entered the room to find Gabriel glowering at both of the women, his arms crossed against his chest.

"Gabriel," Grace said, irritation evident in her voice. "Really, I'm fine. You go with Julia and stay at her house tonight. You hate the couch, and you said the air mattress had a hole in it. Plus, Sam has already peed on your suitcase. He wouldn't leave it alone until you put it in the trunk of your car, remember? He's only going to keep marking it if you bring it in again."

"Sam can sleep outside like dogs are supposed to," Gabriel told her through gritted teeth.

"Absolutely not," Grace replied with a frown. "Sam has never spent the night outside, never in his life."

"Someone needs to take care of you, Grace," Gabriel said, growing exasperated. "You need someone to be with you
130

tonight. Someone broke into your house, and pushed you down the stairs in less than forty-eight hours."

"I'll be there tonight, Michaels," Ren said. Grace turned towards the sound of his voice, and she gave him that same little sad half smile. "I want to check out her house anyway." Gabriel gave him a suspicious look. Ren released an aggravated sigh.

"Good Lord, I'm not going to jump her the minute they release her from the hospital," he said. "I can control my baser instincts." He glanced at Grace to see how she reacted to his comment, and noticed her face had colored an adorable shade of pink. He smiled his first real smile since getting the call. "Besides," he said, shifting his attention back to her brother. "I don't want Julia to be alone. The doctor is pretty sure she was pushed down those stairs, and in case Julia here is wrong about her assumption, Dawson really doesn't like her. If it was him, he could go after her."

Okay, it was a stupid argument, but for some unknown reason, he wanted to be the one to pamper Grace, comfort her, without an overprotective brother breathing down his neck.

"Jules, is your father still over your house?" Gabriel asked, without taking his eyes off of Ren.

"He was going to head out tonight," she said.

Gabriel's gazed flickered with surprise, then hardened. "Okay, but I want a call if anything happens." He walked over to the side of Grace's bed and smiled down at her. "You let Morello take care of you, or I'll call Mom and Dad." He bent down and kissed her unbruised cheek.

Julia slid around him, kissed the same cheek, and gave Grace a gentle hug. She whispered something in her ear that made Grace snort. "You rest," she said more loudly. "I'll come over tomorrow."

Gabriel followed her out of the room, giving Ren a meaningful glance as they headed out the door.

Grace heaved a relieved sigh. "Thank the Lord. I thought they would never leave."

"All your paperwork is done," Ren said. "You need to get dressed so we can get out of here. I'll get a nurse to help you."

She smiled at him and he headed out the door, trying to tamp down on all the protectiveness threatening to swamp him. As he walked to the nurse's station, he tried to remember why he wanted to.

౭౦ౘ

Gabriel chanced a glance over at Julia, who sat next to him in his car. She'd been silent as a stone since they'd left the hospital. He pulled up to the curb in front of the house and saw her father packing his trunk. She stepped out of the car and he followed her. Waves of anger slithered off of her. Slowly, but with purpose, she strode up the walk to her front door. Her father turned, barely gave her a glance and closed his trunk.

"Well, I see you finally decided to make it home." Green eyes, as hard as the emeralds they resembled, glanced over at Gabriel. "Gabriel." Gabriel nodded an acknowledgment. Walter's gaze hardened as it moved back to his daughter. "I take it you haven't reconsidered my offer."

"I thought I was supposed to marry Hubert not you, Walter," Julia said sarcastically. He studied her with those cold, hard eyes for a moment, and then headed to his car door.

"You leave me no choice, young lady. I'm cutting you off."

Gabriel started to step forward, ready to defend her. But the look in Julia's eyes stopped him and left him cold. Never in his life had he observed such distance in her eyes. Hatred, so cold it turned her eyes to stone, sent a shiver down his spine.

"You actually thought threatening me with money was going to get what you wanted," Julia said to her father. She paused, taking a breath, allowing the hate and pain to seep into her belly. It hardened her heart and tore her soul to shreds, but she would survive. She always had. "God, you disgust me. What I really wonder is if you held some kind of an auction for me. Did I go to the highest bidder or to the one with the most connections?"

Her father didn't bat an eye, didn't even show any regret for the loss of a relationship with his daughter. He said, in a voice devoid of all emotion, "You're just like your mother." With that, he got in his car and left.

Julia walked to her front door, and never spared her father a glance as he headed down her street and out of her life. She knew after so many years of indifference it shouldn't hurt, but it did.

When she was younger, especially after living with Grace's family, she dreamed of the perfect father. She had wanted a father who showed up at recitals and graduations, someone who loved her for herself, never questioning whether his daughter was an asset to his life.

She was ashamed to admit to herself that she had envied Grace, but she had and she still did. Oh, Bert had always treated her as if she was his daughter, but she knew, with all her heart, that she longed for that affection from her own father. *After thirty-three years of rejection, you would think I'd have learned,* she thought. The little jabs of bitterness always pierced her heart, no matter how many times she told herself it didn't matter.

She made it to her room before she started to break. Her father saw her as a commodity, a way to advance his companies. She shut the door, slowly slid down the wall and collapsed on the floor. Then, alone as always, she sobbed.

ഈന്ദ

Gabriel stood on the path to Julia's front door and watched the taillights from Walter's car. In all the years he'd known Julia, Gabriel had never known her to be so cold or distant. And, if he was being honest with himself, he'd like to kick the shit out of her father. How could a man who was so intelligent not see what a treasure she was?

Okay, so discovering she was a writer, a writer he admired and envied, may have colored Gabriel's judgment. But Walter was a man who had known her all her life. He'd just cut off the last person in the world who loved him for himself. Gabriel shook his head and walked to the front door.

Once inside, he searched for Julia. He couldn't find her in her living room or kitchen, so he headed back to her bedroom. As he neared the door, heart-wrenching sobs tore at his heart. With any other woman, it would have been bad enough, but this woman never showed any outward emotion, except with his family. Anger surged in his blood. He wanted to chase her father down, drag him out of the car, and beat him to a bloody pulp.

He knocked on her door. The sobs stopped immediately, silencing into sniffles. He waited for her to answer him, but a weighted silence permeated the air. "I'm not going away until you talk to me," he said.

"Go away, Gabriel."

"No."

"I'll be out in a while, Gabriel." Her voice was still hoarse from the sobbing, and he relented.

"As long as you know we are going to talk about this."

He headed to her office and decided he wanted to learn a little bit more about Julia. And if he wanted to do that, he realized, he'd have to acquaint himself with her alter ego, Genevieve Dubois. With no feeling of guilt, he turned on her computer and prepared to invade her privacy.

ॐ

Grace sat in the passenger seat of Ren's truck with her head back and her eyes closed. Every time he glanced at her, the streetlights cast a pallor to her skin he knew wasn't as bad in reality, but it still irritated him. Hell, anger boiled so hot in his blood he worried what he would do when he found out who had pushed her down those stairs. He pulled into his driveway. "Grace," he said in a husky whisper. "Honey, we need to get you in the house."

She smiled then opened her eyes. She looked around in confusion. "What are we doing here?"

"I think you need stay with me tonight. As soon as I get you into the house, I'll go get your mutt."

The smile returned, but a with a seductive edge. "So, you were lying to Gabriel?" It took him a second or two, then he remembered his comment about jumping her bones.

"No. It's probably safer at my house." Okay, a stupid argument, but even he could not explain the surge of protectiveness threatening to black out any of the good intentions he had. She wrinkled her nose at the stupid suggestion. Okay, so even she knew it didn't ring true. Maybe she would take pity on him, and let it pass.

"You mean your house, across the street from mine, is safer?"

No luck. He had no luck when it came to fooling women.

"Your house was broken into yesterday. You have to admit that."

That cute little crease formed between her eyebrows like every time she was thinking. Before he knew what he was doing, he leaned over and kissed the little wrinkle. Surprised, she looked up. Then, her lips curved into a smile full of warmth and sex that shot right down to his gut. Electricity crackled between them. Her lips parted as if waiting for a kiss. Craving but not taking her had been driving him insane. He wanted her with a need that bordered on sexual obsession. He was in serious trouble, but there was nothing he could do.

His hand slid to the nape of her neck, and tangled in those amber curls as he drew the two of them close. The minute his lips touched hers, he knew he'd lost the battle. Her lips were cool and dry, but this time he hadn't surprised her. She had seen the kiss coming, and returned it with enthusiasm. His tongue tickled the line of her sealed lips, and she opened them without hesitation, moaning in appreciation.

His other hand found her breast, and as he plundered her mouth, he massaged and kneaded. The fabric of her jacket hindered his exploration. Without breaking the kiss, his hand slid down the front, unbuttoning it. Once undone, his hand stole inside her jacket and he realized she wore nothing beneath but a bra, one of those lacy half-cup ones that pushed up her breasts. His finger traced the edge, while lightly skimming her flesh that pressed against it. He ignored the fact that his hand shook when he touched her. He teased her by sliding his finger into the cup and gliding it over her nipple. His balls tightened as he moved his finger to the strap, and pulled it down off her shoulder. One extra little tug, and her breast sprang free.

She broke off the kiss, allowing her head to tip back, her eyes still closed. His lips traveled down her exposed throat, flicking his tongue against her hot flesh while his finger began to trace a circle around her nipple. She moaned, an earthy, sensual sound that slid into his stomach and down his spine. Completely genuine, that one little moan was one of the most erotic sounds he'd ever heard.

He continued the descent down her neck to her chest and was within centimeters of devouring her nipple. There wasn't much light inside his truck, but he could make out the puckered bud in the weak glow from one of the nearby streetlights. Blood rushed to his cock. He groaned, and took the nipple into his mouth. He suckled and licked, and her moans increased.

A different beam of light shone through the back window of the truck. Grace let out a groan that skittered through his system. He decided to ignore it.

"Grace," a soft female voice said. "Are you in there?"

Somewhere in his hormone-soaked mind, he recognized that voice. He lifted his head and looked at Grace. Her jacket was undone, her bra half off, and her beautiful rosy-brown nipple glistened from his kiss.

Reason warred with hormones. Reason finished a distant second. He bent his head to take the nipple in his mouth again, when he heard the voice again, only much closer this time.

Then it clicked. That soft, southern voice belonged to the woman he'd rented his house from: Adrienne Michaels, with whom he'd spoken on the phone frequently enough to recognize by voice. He abruptly lifted his head.

"Grace, honey, your mother is standing at the rear of the truck with a flashlight," he said as he pulled the bra strap back up on Grace's shoulder, and had to work the cup back up over that beautiful puckered nipple. He couldn't help himself, and brushed the back of his knuckles over it, happy to see a rush of goose bumps across her chest. Hastily he buttoned her jacket, and looked at her.

"My mother?" she asked, her voice was still husky with passion. The implication of what he said registered and her eyes widened. "My mother?" Her voice raised in worry. Her smile disappeared. "What the hell is my mother doing here?" The last question came out in a whisper, and she crouched down in her seat, trying to hide.

"I have no idea."

As he reached for the door handle, her mother said, "Grace Beatrice Michaels, get out of there right now!"

Chapter Eleven

"Beatrice?" Ren asked.

Grace threw him a look of impatience. "Shut up." Her voice was still coming out in a hoarse whisper. She still crouched behind her seat. She had slunk so low, he was sure she would be on the floor next.

"Renaldo Morello, I know that's you," Adrienne said. "Get out of there this instant."

Grace snorted. "Renaldo."

He frowned. "Shut your pie hole, Beatrice."

She snorted again. He glanced towards the back window of his truck camper and saw Adrienne, with her hands cupped around her face and pressed against the window, trying in vain to see through the tinted glass.

Grace was reaching for the door handle, but he stalled her by touching her arm. "I'll come around and let you out." She turned her head and her mouth opened her mouth to argue. "Listen, despite what I proved by groping you just now, you had a very serious spill down the steps. You need help."

"Okay," she said with a pout. "But you won't pick me up again. You might strain your back."

He rolled his eyes, got out to the vehicle, and walked around the front. He opened her door and before she could argue, he lifted her with no problem. Even in the weak light, he could see Adrienne pale and she dropped the flashlight she had been shining into his truck.

"Grace!" she exclaimed. "What happened, baby?"

"She took a spill down the stairs at the library on campus," Ren said. He started to walk across the street, and noticed an RV was sitting at the curb in front of Grace's house. He knew they must have just pulled up, because he would have noticed something as big as an RV well before now. And of course, while he was attacking Grace in the front seat, he'd never even heard them.

"Mom, you don't need to worry about it," Grace said. "Ren is taking care of everything."

"Janey never said anything about you being hurt," her mother said, keeping pace with Ren as he crossed the street. He heard Grace grumble something under her breath that sounded something like "it figures," but he let it go. All the lights in the front of her house were on. The screen door opened and slammed shut. Sam was left behind, barking loud enough to wake the whole neighborhood as her father rushed toward them, worry etching his features.

Bert Michaels was a little over six feet tall, and still in the shape that had made him a top-notch drill instructor. His thick brown hair was cut military short, but there were a few strands of gray at the temple. His eyes, the same whiskey color as Grace's, were clouded with worry.

"Grace, what happened? Who did this to you?" he asked, giving Ren a suspicious look.

"Hey," he said, feeling a little indignant. "I'm just bringing her home from the hospital."

"Bert," Adrienne said in a soothing voice, as if she spoke to a child. "Go in and let Sam out back. That way Ren can get Grace settled without the dog jumping on her." She put her arm through his, and started walking to the front door. Apparently sensing his indecision, she added, "Then we'll find out what happened, but first we have to take care of Grace."

℘ℭ

Julia splashed cold water on her face, hoping to diminish the swelling in her eyes. She wiped her cheeks with a towel, and looked in the mirror. All of her makeup had come off while she'd been crying, her skin was blotchy, and her eyes were swollen and red. But nothing in her appearance bothered her as much as Gabriel hearing her cry.

From an early age, she'd known her mother had masked the sound of her crying by shoving a towel in her mouth to muffle the sobs. Every time her father had lit into her, Rachel Jacobs had never even flinched. She shoved all of the pain, and disillusionment of a woman who thought she'd married for love deep down into her soul. Julia was convinced that was what eventually helped kill her. Cancer had been the disease that ravaged her body, but she hadn't had much fight left in her. Years of being married to Walter had destroyed her.

Knowing that he would not be put off much longer, Julia decided to face Gabriel. She just knew if he showed her any pity, she would crack again. After searching for him in his room, the kitchen, and the living room and still not finding him, she thought he had decided to be thoughtful and leave the house to give her a break. She walked down the hall to her office, and before she reached it, she noticed light pouring out of the open door. She realized that Gabriel had broken her one rule. He was in her office. Panic welled up in her chest.

When she reached the door, she found him sitting behind her desk, with her computer on, reading what looked like the rough draft of her next novel. Anger replaced panic in a split second.

"About time you got done crying." He didn't even turn around. He just sat there, invading her privacy, touching her things.

"What the hell do you think you are doing?" she asked.

He looked up from the computer, and gave her the same charming smile that had made girls in their high school melt.

"You have a lot of typos here, Jules. I take this is a rough draft?" His voice was light, as if discussing the weather. He turned his attention back to the monitor. "When were you going to tell me that you were Genevieve Dubois?" The light tone was gone. Anger deepened his voice. "Let me guess, you never planning on letting me in, were you? Why not, Julia? Why?"

"Nobody but Grace and my editor know," she said, her voice wooden.

"Dammit, Julia! You have been writing for over ten years and you never thought to tell me?"

"I don't owe you an explanation," she said, sitting in one of the chairs that faced her desk. She closed her eyes and rubbed her temples. "When I left Dallas after college, I really didn't need to work. My mother left me a trust fund, so despite what Walter thinks or says, I don't need his money. I really didn't know what to do with myself. The only thing open to spoiled little rich girls was charity work, being on committees and stuff like that. I just didn't have the patience.

"I'd been writing since high school, so I decided to try that full-time. Everything else came the old-fashioned way, as I'm sure you know. Mountains of rejection letters. Revisions, rewrites and resubmissions. I finally landed a good agent and she got me a good deal for my first book. I made enough to earn back my advance and then some, and even made the *USA Today* bestseller list. The rest, as they say, is history."

She opened her eyes to find him looking at her with a warm look and a slight smile.

"Yeah, *ancient* history," he said. "I understand why you might not have wanted to tell me about it to begin with, but Julia, it's been ten years." When she shot him a look, he rolled his eyes. "What am I thinking? You two can't go to the bathroom without telling one another. Of course she knows."

"Gabriel," she said, trying to avoid what she knew was inevitable.

He was not going to let it go. "Julia, we are going to have this out here and now. I'm not letting you go before you tell me—why the secrecy?"

Her green eyes narrowed in anger and she said, her voice low and controlled, the Texan accent more pronounced, "Because Walter would never approve of me being a writer," she said. "And I'd never hear the end of it from him if he found out I wrote erotic thrillers."

"Okay," Gabriel said. "I can understand that. But why in the world you wouldn't tell me. Gabriel, your old buddy. The other writer, you know." The last was said through clenched teeth.

"I didn't want you to think any less of me than you already do."

He was a little surprised, and he had to admit, thrilled that she cared what he thought of her. Since he had first noticed her, when she was fourteen to his seventeen, he had always felt drawn to her. Her cool demeanor, however, had stalled any thoughts of a relationship, even when she was old enough. He had been back for a weekend from TCU when she had gotten home, disheveled and an hour late from a date with Jimmy Callandar. It hadn't taken a genius to figure out what she'd been up to. By Sunday night, Jimmy had made sure that everyone in town had known he had melted the Ice Maiden. Gabriel had been so hurt, angry, and misguided in his belief that she should have waited for him, so he locked away any feelings he had for Julia, and had kept her at a distance ever since.

"So, contrary from the way you act, you care about what I think of you," he said. "That's really interesting." He got up and walked around the desk. "It's most peculiar, because the first thing I felt when I found out who you were wasn't anger, but hurt, Julia. I mean, if there's one thing in this world I understand it's this love for something that drives you and won't let you let it go."

"Other than my agent, editor and Grace, you're the only one who knows. I only tell those I trust."

"And you don't trust me?"

"You don't understand anything, Gabriel," she snapped with a frown. "Least of all about me. You're just like everyone else, every other man—quick to judge and even quicker to *mis*-judge."

He sat down in the chair next to her, and said in a quiet voice, "Who hurt you, Julia? Who shattered your trust in men?"

She looked at him with those sad green eyes that just about swallowed her face, and then her gaze shifted away. "Name a man in my life, excluding your father, and you've got your culprit." He tugged on her hand until she looked at him. "I knew from the time I was nine that Walter kept a mistress in Dallas. When my parents would fight, he wouldn't hesitate to remind my mother, and he didn't care if I was around to hear the conversation. I didn't even know at the time what a mistress was. I just knew that when he mentioned it, it hurt my mother. He also blamed her for his lack of an heir. He has always been disappointed that I'm not a man."

"Is that the only reason you don't like your father, Jules?" he asked, his voice just above a whisper.

"What, I need another one?" she said with a dismissive tone.

"I don't know," he replied. "You tell me. This mistrust you feel for everybody, about everything...it seems to go deep. Way deeper than your dad's affair, Julia."

She looked away, cutting her eyes across the room. "I'm not letting this go," he said. "I want to know who hurt you so badly that you want nothing to do with men. And we are not leaving this room until you tell me."

Chapter Twelve

Sunlight filtered through the blinds, dappling Julia's ivory skin. She lay on her stomach, her head facing away from him. Gabriel pulled the red sheet down. All that ivory skin against the crimson amazed him, as did the sheets themselves. Cool, distant Julia Jacobs had a streak of passionate wickedness. A black comforter had covered her king-sized bed, but the surprise had been all of that red silk he'd discovered beneath.

When they had finally had their talk last night, he'd been heartbroken. All of those years he'd thought that she'd slept willingly with Jimmy Callander, and in truth, Jimmy had raped her. She'd returned to the Michaels' home after her assault, disheveled, frightened and distraught, and he'd offered her nothing but disdain. No comfort, no shoulder to cry on, nothing.

I'm an ass, he'd thought. With that revelation, he'd been afraid to move forward, not wanting to scare her. But she hadn't even paused. She'd led him down the hall to her room and allowed him to take the lead in reintroducing her to passion. He smiled as he traced circles on her back. Sex seemed too insignificant a word for what they'd just shared. Images of the night before, her soft skin, her moans, the way it felt to slide his cock into her tight vagina, nudged his usual arousal into a full-blown erection.

She stirred, her hand coming around to swat at him as if he were a pesky bug. Her head shifted on her pillow, turning to face him. Once again, he was amazed at her beauty. His heart tumbled when he realized he could wake up looking at this face for the rest of his life. Age could add lines and gray to her hair. He wouldn't care. This woman was his soul mate, the one person who could make him complete. He leaned over and kissed a line down her spine, inhaling the musky scent of her skin.

"Just because I was nice to you last night doesn't mean you can bother me today, Michaels," she said. Her voice, husky with slumber, sent another wave of lust through his system. Her sultry Texas accent and her cool demeanor reminded him of hot skin and cool ice.

"Says who?" he asked between kisses. He leaned back and looked at her. "You just better get used to it, Jules."

She opened her mouth to argue when the doorbell rang. He raised an eyebrow in question and she shrugged. "It could be Walter. He could be back to propose again."

Before he even thought about it, Gabriel jumped off the bed, and grabbed the comforter, wrapping it around him. He stormed out of her bedroom and down the hall to the front door. If that jackass thought he could marry his woman off to some corporate asshole, he had another thing coming. He reached the front door, yanked it open and found Ren Morello on the porch. Confusion came first to the police chief's eyes, then comprehension and finally humor.

"What do you want, Morello?"

"I thought I'd come by to tell you two to get over to Grace's house for lunch. We're going to go over everything and hope to come up with a list of suspects. I tried calling, but all I got was a busy signal." Ren looked over Gabriel's shoulder and his smile widened. "Morning, Goulia."

Gabriel glanced over his shoulder and saw Julia in nightshirt that stopped at mid-thigh, exposing her long lean legs and all that ivory skin. It was ten-thirty. If he played it right, he could have a few more hours with those legs wrapped around his waist, his dick buried deep within her.

People ate lunch at three in the afternoon, didn't they?

"Oh, and Michaels, your parents got here last night." That jerked him back to reality and he turned to face Morello. "Seems Ms. Janey decided to give them a call."

Silently, Gabriel cursed. He didn't need his parents interfering with Julia and him.

"Thanks. Is that the only reason you stopped by?" he asked, slowly closing the door.

"Gabriel! Maybe Ren wants to have some coffee." Julia tried to step around him. Gabriel was ready to rip off the comforter to cover her, not caring about his nudity when Morello's reply stopped him.

"No, thanks anyway. I need to stop by the office, see if they turned anything up last night." He shifted his gaze to Gabriel. "I'll be there at noon. That should give you plenty of time." He touched the brim of the hat and turned to walk away.

Gabriel shut the door and looked at Julia. Those green eyes sparked with anger. She was tapping her foot, her hands on her hips. He was ready to take her against the wall and screw her until she couldn't see straight.

"Why is the phone busy?" she asked.

"I took it off the hook around three this morning." He didn't even trying to hide his smile.

She sighed and ran a hand through her hair. "I guess we need to get ready and head over."

He looked at her for a moment, saying nothing. Then he took two steps forward, leaned over, and hiked her up over his shoulder. "Nope, we have at least an hour." He headed back to her bedroom.

"No, no way, Gabriel. I need a shower."

Before he could drop her on her bed, he turned and headed to her bathroom. "Great! There's that shower scene I read last night from your manuscript that I want to try."

ₔℛ

Grace sat in her big comfy chair with a notepad in her lap. She was trying to list anything that could have happened to her in the last few months. She figured that might help her figure out who hated her enough to push her down the stairs. Trying to concentrate was getting impossible, however. Dr. Meyers and Dr. Gump had finished their lectures for the day, and had appeared on her doorsteps with fresh tomatoes and sympathy. Several people had dropped off dishes filled with casseroles, including something from Lorna Peterson that looked like noodles but it had been hard to tell.

Julia and Gabriel had showed up a few minutes earlier. Julia had been acting kind of strange. Grace wanted to get her into a corner to question her, but found herself too lazy to get up and move. Sam, the traitor, was busy begging for scraps from her father.

The doorbell rang, bringing Sam out of his lust for food. His boisterous barks began to bring back the pounding in her head. She closed her eyes and tried to block out the pain. Ren's rich deep voice reached her, and she opened her eyes. A tingle of warmth slid down her spine. Her father led Ren into the living room and she smiled at him, receiving only an aloof and lukewarm response. The slight distance in his eyes she'd witnessed when she first met him had returned and bewildered, she drew in a deep breath.

"I've been making some notes," she said. "I figured if I thought hard enough I might be able to come up with something to help you." She held up the spiral notebook for him to read, satisfied she had kept her tone light, and had controlled the slight shake in her hands. "Not much happened other than you moving in, Darian showing up and my research."

She swallowed hard as he took the notebook without even looking at her. Dr. Meyers, probably sensing her distress, came and sat on the arm of her chair.

"I told Grace she needed to trace the Cannon family," he said. "We had all thought that Willie Cannon's daughters left no heirs, but one did. She died under mysterious circumstances." He took her hand into his, squeezing it. "Some people don't want information like that to get out about their family."

Ren's concentration moved from Dr. Meyers back to her. "What kind of information would that be?"

She took another swallow to stop the tremor in her voice. Didn't he realize his cold tone hurt her?

She went on to explain everything she knew so far about the Cannons and their patriarch, Cord McPherson. Her recitation of the facts took about ten minutes. If she had to spend five more minutes with Ren acting so indifferently, she knew she would break down. "That's all I know. I figure what I need to do is start looking into this third sister and her children. That may give us a lead."

"I think you can just leave that to me," Ren said, his tone professional and distant.

"Excuse me, but this is my research, and I will do whatever I damn well please." She struggled to her feet. "My head is hurting and I need to get some rest. Julia, could you get my drugs out of the kitchen?"

Grace didn't say goodbye to anyone as Gabriel helped her upstairs.

ഇറ

Ren discussed a little more of the Cannon family history with Dr. Meyers and Dr. Gump. The hurt look in Grace's golden brown eyes had pained him almost physically. That brilliant smile had faded when she noticed his coldness, but he couldn't do anything about that. He had to solve this case to protect her, and to protect her he had decided to distance himself. So, even if his chest ached when he saw the shuttered look in her eyes, he would ignore it.

After thanking the professors for their help, he headed to the front door. "Ren," Adrienne said from behind him. "Are you alright? You seem out of sorts."

"Yes," he said with a tight smile as he turned to her. "I'm okay. It's just a little hard dealing with the case. I need to be professional."

She returned a smile, but hers was relaxed and full of warmth. "I know, Ren. Grace may not understand, but I do. You just find the person who did this to my daughter." He nodded and headed out the door. "Oh, and Ren?"

He turned to face her once more. "I'll accept what you are doing is for her own good, but if you hurt my baby for another reason, I'll let Gabriel and Bert take care of you."

He smiled—a real smile this time—and said, "That would be your right, Adrienne."

∞∞

Over the next few days, Ren discovered he could function without sleep. All of his time at work and home he spent researching the Cannon family. Sleep was minimal, because when he slept, he found himself dreaming about Grace. He would awake from the erotic dreams, with a ten-foot boner and no one to relieve it but himself. But each time he cursed her existence and his attraction to her, he remembered the pain he'd witnessed in her eyes before she hid it from him.

He'd discovered Charlotte Cannon married Ned Langdon in 1907, had two children and died under mysterious circumstances. Although there'd been reports that her husband had killed her, the official report had been suicide. Shortly after the mess, Ned Langdon, probably trying to shield his children from the rumors, had moved down to Laredo. That's where the trail grew cold. Ren had a feeling that Langdon might have changed his last name. Pretty easy to do in those days, considering the state of official records.

He also checked out Dawson, but not only had he been with Ronnie, the desk-hopping research assistant at the time of Grace's assault, they had actually been at the Wagon Wheel Restaurant. More than two-dozen people accounted for both of them.

Ren still had a few feelers out to some local lawmen in south Texas, but by Friday, he was feeling the strain of responsibility. He hated to admit part of that was steering clear of Grace.

He had broodingly watched as she left for work each day, but reassured himself that it was to make sure that she wasn't driving. That was the only reason. It had nothing to do with the fact he missed seeing her, and talking to her. He was sure he really didn't miss that twinkle in her eye each time she smiled, and that little wrinkle that formed each time she frowned. And it definitely had nothing to do with missing her husky laughter that always sounded like it should be floating out of a bedroom.

The only reason he stood behind the curtains, sneaking a peek at her like he was some kind of stalker, was for her safety. It definitely was not for his peace of mind.

He rubbed the back of his neck, trying to work out the kinks, and decided to call it a night. He decided to swing by the college to make sure Grace had left for the day.

He had to. It was part of his job.

Chapter Thirteen

Against her parents' wishes, Grace returned to teaching on Wednesday. She couldn't handle sitting around the house, not doing anything. So she went through the motions, happy that in both classes she gave tests Wednesday. That also meant someone else could have taken care of it, but her parents were driving her crazy. If either one of them patted her hand or asked how she was doing one more time, she was sure she'd scream.

Since she was still not supposed to drive, her father dropped her off and Gabriel picked her up. Julia had told Grace about their burgeoning relationship. He was still staying with Julia, and other than Grace telling him it didn't matter if he was her brother, that she would hurt him if he hurt Julia, she let the matter go.

At night, to escape her parents, she isolated herself in her room, pouring over Suzanna Cannon's diary. Thanks to some information Ren had dropped off, conveniently while she was working, she had found out that Suzanna's mysterious sister Charlotte's married name was Langdon. She knew Ren was checking out that end of it, but she really thought he was chasing a red herring. The Cannons were all gone, their descendants all dead. There was no way someone kin to them could have learned about her research, must less tried to put a stop to it.

She sat reading the diary, and waited for Gabriel. He was late picking her up again, she thought with a grin. She would have been mad if she weren't sure he was preoccupied with Julia.

Besides, she'd arrived at an interesting point in the diary, where Suzanna wrote in vivid description about a wedding she'd attended. She included everything, right down to the something borrowed.

The phone rang, pulling her out of her study.

"Grace," Dr. Maryanne Foster said in a desperate voice. "You have to come out tonight." Maryanne was a professor in the English department. She always sounded desperate.

"No, I don't. Remember, I'm recovering. You know, that silly little thing about me falling down the stairs."

"Yes, I remember. You should be more careful," Maryanne said.

Grace tried to ignore the anger boiling beneath her skin. "I was pushed," she said between clenched teeth.

"Sure, Grace," Maryanne said. "But this important. That author we had speak at the writing center is leaving tomorrow and we're taking him out to experience the Texas nightlife at The Well."

"And this is important to me because...?"

"I want you to come. Most of the other professors are married. It's going to leave me at the table with him and he has fifteen hands."

"Once again I ask, why is this important to me?" She was about to tell Maryanne there was no way she would step foot in The Well when her office door opened. She looked up, expecting to find Gabriel, but saw Ren instead. His face was grim. He walked determinedly toward her desk.

"I'll tell you what," she said. "I have to go home and change. I'll also need a ride if I can't get Gabriel and Julia to go."

"Great! Give me a call on my cell if you do," Maryanne said. "We're meeting there around nine. I can pick you up on my way."

After agreeing, Grace hung up. "Did you find out anything new?" she asked Ren, allowing the pain in her heart to come out cool in her voice. He had hurt her feelings terribly with his cool rebuke at her house, and she knew he'd been purposely avoiding her ever since. She didn't understand why, but she wouldn't be like some women and cry and complain. She was a mature professional.

Ignoring her question, Ren said, "I was driving by and saw your lights on. You really shouldn't be here by yourself."

She leaned back in her chair, and crossed her arms beneath her breasts. If she didn't hide her hands, the anger she felt would surely show. When she got mad, and she did have a real temper, her hands shook, and she cried.

How dare this jerk show up in her office, pretending to care about what happened to her? If he really cared, he would have explained why he was treating her as if she had a highly communicable disease.

She took a deep breath. "Dr. Gump is still here and Gabriel should be on his way."

Okay, see? That was mature. She didn't tell him to fly a freaking kite and that it wasn't any of his business.

He seemed to mull that over while he casually walked around her office. "You really shouldn't be going out tonight."

He didn't look at her, but at her bookshelves. Shock from his reprimand dissolved quickly to anger. "Oh, and why wouldn't I want do that, Chief Morello?"

He turned to face her, exasperation evident on his face. "Dammit, Grace! It isn't safe for you to go out. You know there's still someone out there who wants to hurt you."

"Oh, I don't know. Maybe you're wrong. Maybe I fell down those stairs, like everyone is saying."

"Grace that's not true. Besides, you're still recovering from that fall. I don't think it's a good idea to be staying out all night on dates."

Okay, that did it. She jumped out of her chair. He backed up a step.

He thought he could come in here, tell her what to do after he trampled all over her feelings? Rage, swift and hot, sped through her, pounded through her veins. She was no longer the mature professional.

"Listen, you ignoramus, I can go out with whomever I want!" She stalked him around her desk. "If I want to date all the professors from the English department—hell, if I want to date the weirdoes over in the electronics division, I can." She poked him in the chest. "You have no right to tell me what I can and can not do. Do you understand me?"

"Grace, I'm sure everyone understands you. I'm sure that everyone within a five-mile radius heard you," Gabriel said from the doorway.

"Oh, shut up, Gabriel!"

Even Gabriel, who had seen her in full temper many times before, looked astonished at the display of anger. She turned to face him, placing her hands on her hips.

"My office and home were broken into, I was pushed down the stairs, my mother caught me necking in the front seat of a truck and now this idiot..." She jerked her thumb in Ren's direction. "...thinks he can tell me what I can do, and who I can date." She dragged in a huge breath. "I've had it. The next person who tells me what to do will lose a limb."

"Grace," Ren said in a warning tone. "I'm not sure…"

"Oh, go fuck yourself Ren."

Did I really say that out loud?

No one said a word; the silence after her tirade hung in the air like lead. She glanced up at Ren's face to see his reaction. He stood there, tall and angry, his chocolate-brown eyes turned as black as coal. The anger hardened his face, and his nostrils flared. Only the sound of his angry breath filled the office.

"I think I'll let you take care of this one, Morello. Make sure she gets home," Gabriel said, waiting for a nod from Ren. If she had not been studying him so closely, she would have missed it. "Good luck, Grace."

And then he deserted her. Her favorite brother, her only brother, deserted her with one really pissed Chief of Police. She was going to rethink letting Julia get involved with him. And she really had to talk to her folks about disowning him.

"Okay," she said, as if she was dealing with a homicidal maniac.

When she saw the anger on Ren's face and his fists clenched, she was pretty sure she was.

"I really didn't mean anything by that silly little comment."

He didn't say a word. His anger flowed off him so intensely, she stepped back. Maybe she had gone a little far.

But, hey, how much could a girl take? She'd never been so humiliated as when he'd treated her like she disgusted him. She hadn't slept well, even when she gave into the pain and took a pill.

Ever since her relationship with Darian, she'd been sure that maybe there was something wrong with her. She hadn't been able to respond to Darian in all the months she had been with him. But all Ren had to do was look at her, and lust coiled deep in her belly. And his kisses! Lust boiled to the surface, threatening to explode when he touched her with that wicked mouth of his. But now, he acted like he didn't want her. He wanted to tell her what she could do, but he didn't want her.

He had no right to tell her if she could go out with someone. He had kissed her, caressed her, bringing her to the brink of consummation, and then dropped her. Her temper boiled to the surface again and she placed her hands on her hips, and met him stare for stare. He didn't say a word. He just grabbed her wrist, and started pulling her toward her door.

"Ren, wait, I need my coat and the diary."

He turned, grabbed the book off of her desk, her coat and her purse and pulled her out the door, slamming it behind him. He stood waiting, and she chanced a look up at his face. "Lock the door, Grace." A shimmer of barely controlled rage vibrated in his deep voice.

She turned to lock the door, which was hard because he wouldn't let go of her wrist. With only one hand, she couldn't steady the doorknob. He released an exaggerated sigh, dropped her wrist, and grabbed the keys from her with an angry jerk. He locked the door, pocketed the keys, and captured her wrist in the painful grip again. Without a backward glance to make sure she would follow, he stalked down the hall, pulling her in his wake. If he grabbed her by the hair and dragged her down the hall like some kind of cave man, she wouldn't be surprised.

Anyone who might have been listening to the conversation had scattered like cowards. There was no one to save her. To keep pace with his long-legged stride, she had to double her steps. She didn't know where he was dragging her, but she was pretty sure telling the Chief of Police to fuck off wasn't against the law, so he wasn't taking her to jail.

He shoved the building door open, and a blast of cold wind smacked her in the face. Ren never showed any discomfort. He just walked on, ignoring her. She wasn't going to worry. He would calm down by the time they got to where they needed to go. She was sure he wouldn't kill her. Well, pretty sure.

₮℞

Ren pulled into Grace's driveway, still furious. How could Grace have said a thing like that? Okay, so maybe he'd pushed her a little far by giving her orders. But he'd been justified. How could she be going out tonight, four nights after being attacked, four nights since he'd almost taken her in the front seat of this very truck? Didn't it mean anything to her? Couldn't she see he was doing this for her own safety?

It occurred to him when she was poking him with her finger, he had never been so aroused in his entire life. Grace might like to transmit to the world that she was quiet and professional, but one peek at her temper, and most people would know it was a façade. He realized when she was yelling at him that he had never seen her mad. He had seen her a little upset, but never in a temper. Anger had stripped away the cool composed professor, and left behind a woman who vibrated passion with each angry breath she took.

That redheaded, Irish temper had caused her eyes to spark gold in anger, and her body had shaken. When she'd yelled at him, the only thing he could think of was being on top of her, and inside of her, as she acted out all that passion. There was no way he was going to let her go out with some faceless professor now. He'd brought all that temper to forefront, and he deserved to reap the benefits. She sat, her arms crossed beneath her breasts, looking straight ahead, breathing heavily as if she was trying to calm down. Well, one way or another, they were going to have this out, right now.

He got out, and slammed his door behind him. Grace got out and slammed her door even harder. Damn, she was a sight to see. Half of the curls she had secured behind her head that morning had tumbled down. Her temper caused a flush on her cheeks. Anger warred with arousal as he watched her stalk toward him, her sensible pumps tapping out an angry cadence. She carried the diary in the crook of her arm.

"Grace?" her mother called across the street.

Without looking at her mother, she said, "Ren and I have a few things to discuss, Mom. I'll be over here." She stalked closer, and he could smell the familiar scent of her musky perfume.

She followed him inside and they went to the kitchen. She slammed the diary down on the counter. Her eyes were golden and that flush was still there.

"Now, you want to tell me what this is all about?" she said, pointing at him. "You were the one who gave me the cold shoulder. I just want to know what the hell you want from me."

He looked at her heaving chest, golden eyes and tangled red curls, and decided he didn't care about anything else but her. Not his hang-ups about commitment and serious relationships, or the fact someone wanted to hurt her. All that mattered was *this* right now. Grace. It had always been Grace.

The control he had worked so hard to foster broke, passion and anger flooding through his senses. He took a step closer, slid his hand around her waist, and brought her body flush with his.

"This."

He backed her up against the kitchen counter, bent his head, and devoured her mouth. The hard ridge of his arousal pressed against her belly. At first, surprise kept her inactive. He'd been so angry. Then his tongue stole past her lips and tangled with hers.

She lifted her leg and stood on her tiptoe, entwining her leg with one of his, and she rubbed against him. He groaned as she began to suck on his tongue. Placing his hand on her thigh, he leisurely began to knead it, moving slowly, sensuously up until he felt the lacy top of her thigh-high stocking. His hand stilled. He pulled back from her, his eyes heavy lidded and his nostrils flared.

"Well, well, well," he said while pulling her skirt higher. When he could finally see where the black silk met her honey-white skin, he shuddered. "You never stop surprising me, Grace." He took a breath as if to steady his nerves. "I have this thing for silk stockings and garters. But these thigh highs are just as good."

Without thinking, she said, "All of my stockings had runs in them."

He quickly looked up and smiled again. "You're killing me here, Grace."

Before Grace had time to think about it, her shirt and skirt were lying in a crumpled heap on the floor, and he had lifted her onto the counter top, bringing her breasts level to his eyes. Her pumps dropped on the kitchen floor with a thud. With nothing but a bra, panties, and her thigh highs on, she felt self-conscious, but resisted the urge to cover herself and hide from him. Without looking up, he slowly, reverently, skimmed the top of her black lace demi bra with his fingers. Chills raced up her arms while heat pooled into her belly.

"Grace," he said, again not looking up. His hot breath warmed her breasts. "You have the body of a goddess. I'm not sure if I'm up to the challenge." His finger dipped in between her breasts. She shivered. "But," he said, moving his fingers to the other cup of her bra. "I'm going to try my damnedest."

His other hand reached around and unhooked her bra. He still hadn't looked up, but he hurriedly pulled the bra off and tossed it on the floor. He bent his head, and took a puckered nipple in his mouth. She groaned, moving her hands into his hair to hold him while he sucked. His other hand moved over to her other nipple, and began kneading her other breast. She tipped her head back while still holding his head in place. He moved over to her other nipple and swirled his tongue around the very tip of it before he took it into his mouth. He shifted and slid his hand down her stomach. The tips of his talented fingers brushed against her dampened curls. He broke away from her breast, and she groaned in protest.

"Damn, Grace, you're so hot and wet." His voice was hoarse with passion. He trailed kisses up her neck and then he was devouring her mouth once again. He began to pull the elastic of her panties back to make room for his fingers when she gave his shoulders a little push. He looked up with surprise in his eyes.

"Don't tell me you want to stop." he said hoarsely.

She licked her lips. "No. You have way too many clothes on."

He pulled back, and started to unbutton his shirt. Impatiently, Grace grabbed the waistband of his pants and started to unzip them. He dropped his shirt on the floor, and stilled her hands. "We have to make it upstairs," he said. "That's not going to happen if you take my pants off."

She pouted. "Why can't we just finish here?" she asked, sliding her hand down his body and cupping his dick, strained against the denim.

"Protection," he gasped as her hand slid back up his body and she caressed one of his nipples. "I don't have anything down here."

She dropped her hand and smacked him on the shoulder. "What are you waiting for?"

He laughed, scooped her up, and she wrapped her legs around his waist. He couldn't believe his luck. Miss Goody Two Shoes turned out to be a sex goddess in disguise. His hands slipped around to cup her ass, and came in contact with bare skin. His heart almost stopped and he nearly dropped her when he realized she wore a thong. All those contrasts and her magnificent breasts pressed against his chest made his blood pound as he raced up the stairs.

Ren dropped her on his bed, shucked out of his jeans and boxers, and came down on top of her. He pressed her into the mattress, reveling in the feel of all her curves and the way they fit against his skin. The scent of her filled his senses. She caught his earlobe between her teeth, and then flicked it with her tongue.

Knowing he was close to losing control, Ren fumbled with his nightstand drawer, yanked it open and grabbed the box of condoms. He juggled it with one hand, and he inserted a finger, pulling it open. Condoms scattered all over the floor. Grace's throaty laugh filled the room. He grabbed one and had it on in record time. He pulled her panties off, and she started roll her stockings down.

He stilled her hand. "No, leave those on."

Grace spread her legs, welcoming him into her warmth. Inch-by-inch, he entered. Her muscles tightly clasped his shaft.

When he was in her to the hilt, he pulled almost all the way out and sunk back in. Damn, she was so tight and wet. Soon, he could no longer hold back and began to speed up his rhythm. Grace met him, thrust for thrust. He held back the best he could, but he knew he was walking a thin edge.

"Come on, baby. Come for me," Ren said.

She entwined his waist with her legs again. Her silk stockings slid against his skin. He pumped into her, forgetting restraint, only trying to achieve the pinnacle. Reaching down between their bodies, he massaged her clit. She moaned his name, her muscles clamping his cock. He continued thrusting, but lifted away to watch her. Her hair was a tangled mass of curls against the pillow, her eyes closed. Her mouth, wet and swollen from his kisses, opened in a silent moan. Just the sight of her, watching her come, brought on his own orgasm.

Chapter Fourteen

Grace lay beneath Ren, her body relaxed and loose. He had yet to move since collapsing on top of her, and she allowed his musky animal heat to surround her and seep into her skin. She stroked her hands up and down his back, thinking she would never be able to get enough of his delicious body. Every fiber of her body, from her big red hair to the tips of her toes, was humming. Virtually humming with satisfaction.

She knew this would never last. Ren liked a different kind of woman, and she really didn't think he wanted to settle down like she did. She'd live in the present. If she never expected anything else, she wouldn't be disappointed, right?

"Well," she said, recognizing the huskiness in her voice. "I think I'll let you win that one."

He finally stirred and lifted off of her, bracing himself on his elbows to look down at her. The autumn sun had started to set outside, bringing shadows to the room, but she could see the white flash of his smile.

"I think we both won that one."

Low and seductive, his warm voice coursed through her. She curled her toes. He rolled onto his back and pulled her up against him, lightly skimming her back with his fingers, descending until he cupped his hand around one cheek and squeezed.

166

"Now you're going to tell me what you think you were doing, going out tonight," he said.

She sat up, completely unself-conscious of her nudity. She took a deep breath, trying to calm her sudden spike in temper. "What do you mean, what do I think I was doing?"

The nerve of the man. He'd pulled out her heart, stomped all over it, then thought he can give her the best sex of her life, and tell her what to do.

Well, okay, I'll take the sex.

"I was talking to a friend, a female friend, when you showed up today. I was invited with a group of people to go out tonight." She held up one her hands to stop his argument. "You had no right to barge into my office, and start ordering me around. I'm not one of your deputies."

"You were attacked the other night—" he began.

"Oh, for the love of God, if that's what this is all about, then I just wasted an hour. Well, not wasted, but definitely not what I thought." She stood and searched the floor for her clothes.

She started to walk out of the room when his arm wrapped around her waist. He pulled her down on the bed. He pinned her arms above her head, and the rest of his hard body anchored hers to the mattress. His long, hard sex pressed her vagina. She was ashamed to admit to herself that it sent shivers of excitement racing up and down her spine.

Ren sighed. "Let us get one thing straight, here. I was worried about you going out because of your injuries, and I really didn't want you going out with some stupid professor." She opened her mouth to protest, but he secured both her hands with one of his, and used the other one to cover her mouth. "Now, you're going to listen to me. I didn't want you running around town at all. If I had my way, I would keep you hog tied."

She humphed against his hand.

"Preferably in my bed," he added. "Also, I have to admit I was jealous. I know I don't have a right, because I treated you so badly, but there it is. I only did it for your own good. When you're around, I can't concentrate. If I can't concentrate, I can't solve this case, and protect you. Jesus, do you think I've been enjoying myself? I haven't had a decent night's sleep since I met you. How can I protect you, and be close to you at the same time?" If anything happened to you, I don't know what I would do. Can't you see that is the reason I tried to stay away from you?"

Did he just admit what I think he did? she thought, startled. Did Ren Morello just tell me in an ass backward way that he cares about me?

"I tried," he told her. "Lord knows I tried to stay away, so I could be objective. But staying away was just too hard. I couldn't resist you."

He kept his hand over her mouth. She tried to say something, her lips moving beneath his hand and her tongue against his palm. He removed his hand, but before she could utter a sound, he replaced it with his mouth.

Grace molded her body to his; chest to breast, belly to stomach, thigh to thigh. The warmth of his flesh seeped through her skin, down to her bones, and warmed her from the inside out. The hand that had covered her mouth cupped the side of her face, and his callused fingers caressed her cheek and the soft skin under her chin.

Her arms slid around his muscled back to embrace him, trying to pull him closer. Gyrating his hips, he rubbed his cock against her wet curls. Lazily, he kissed the underside of her jaw, then her throat, and then pressed his mouth and tongue at the hollow of her neck before moving to her breasts.

Anticipation pulsed through her. He worked his way down her body, kissing and caressing her skin while whispering his admiration for each part he touched. He skimmed wet, hot kisses across her stomach, then pushed her thighs apart and situated his hard, hot body between them.

She propped herself on her elbows, and looked down just in time to see his head descend to place a kiss on the inside of her thigh. She shivered with pleasure. He licked where he had kissed, and worked his way up to her clit. His breath heated her skin and her muscles clenched. An electric shock coursed through her body. Her head dropped back, her hair spilling across the pillows.

He kissed her then, sucking, and licking her clit and folds. Heat seared through her, as he added his finger, continuing the assault of sweet agony and licked her clit. As he took the nub between his teeth, a fire flowed through her, building to a peak that excited and frightened her. Panic, almost as strong as her passion, raced through her. Before she could pull back to protect herself, her orgasm crashed through her and she surrendered to the flood of sensations, forgetting everything but that one moment.

Ren slid back up her body, pausing to lick each nipple. In one powerful thrust, he entered her, eased by the sweet honey of her passion. He groaned her name and captured her lips in a kiss. She could taste her own tangy essence as his tongue slid past her lips and invaded her mouth. His thrusts were powerful but controlled, frustrating her. She met each, desperately trying to increase the speed. His hands slid down her body and anchored her hips to the bed, while continuing the same rhythm. Almost methodically, he stroked her smoldering embers, rekindling the fire, sending flames racing through her blood once again. He released her hips, balanced his weight on his hands, and began pushing so deep she was sure she could feel him touch her womb. In perfect rhythm, she rose to meet each thrust.

"Oh, Grace, baby, now!" He pushed into her one last time, and came. The last thrust sent her over the edge for a second time, her orgasm as powerful as the first.

After a few moments, he lifted himself off of her and rolled onto his back, pulling her across his chest. He disposed of the condom she hadn't realized he'd put on and kissed the top of her head. "We have to slow down, Grace, or you're going to kill me."

He closed his eyes and a moment later, she smiled when he snored. The musky scent of their passion filled the air, and she cuddled closer to him, trying to sink into his body heat. As she thought back about the events, their fight and their lovemaking, a tingling of fear whispered across her mind. She realized in that moment that she loved him. She loved his sense of honor, his dry humor; hell, she even loved him when he was grumpy.

He'd warned her he didn't get serious; he didn't get involved. She'd walked into it with her eyes wide open, and fell flat on her face. Grace sighed and knew that she would love him until the day she died. She would return the passion he so willingly shared and walk away when the time came, even though she knew that her heart would shatter with each step. Knowing she was never one to ignore reality, she accepted the inevitable and drifted into a dreamless sleep.

&)(&

When Ren awoke the next morning, Grace's sweet fragrance filled his senses, and a tumble of auburn curls tickled his chest. His whole face spread into a grin as he thought about the night before. She possessed combustible passion she hid beneath ugly suits and controlled tones. Anyone looking at her for the first time would take in the conservative dress and hair, and miss the fire that burned beneath her skin, and the embers that glowed in those golden eyes.

He glanced over at his nightstand to check the time, and noticed the numerous foil wrappers that littered the surface. Each time they'd awoke, they'd come together in such a frenzy, he had almost forgotten to use a condom a couple of times.

Silently, Ren counted the wrappers and was amazed to find six. The last time he had stirred, she had pressed that sweet, luscious ass against his groin. He'd caressed and teased her, and before she was completely awake, he had entered her from behind. The sex had been over in a matter of minutes, and Grace had drifted back to sleep almost immediately, but he'd lingered over her body, kissing and caressing her until he fell asleep. Just thinking about her cunt clamping tight around his dick tightened his balls.

His smile widened when he spotted her black stockings hanging over the footboard where he had thrown them, after he used his teeth to strip them off of her during one of their sessions. She was all curves and soft skin, with breasts designed for exploration. Her belly was gently rounded and had a smattering of freckles around her belly button. It had been dark last night, but now he hoped for a chance to search for more freckles.

She stirred, shifting her weight from one side to the other, as if trying to find a comfortable spot. A tingling of excitement raced through him as her hand trailed sensuously down his stomach, and encircled his morning hard-on. Her fingers wrapped around him firmly, and she stroked him once then turned her head to look up at him with a smile.

"Good morning," he said, his tone husky.

She smiled, then turned her head and pressed her lips to his chest. She planted tantalizing open-mouth kisses in a line traveling down his stomach and scorched a blazing inferno through his soul. She paused as she reached his throbbing shaft. A whisper of her sweet breath warmed his skin the moment before she took him in her mouth. Ren fell back against his pillow, closing his eyes, and grabbing fistfuls of sheets. She kept stroking with her hand as she slid her tongue around the tip of his sex. Then she slid his cock into her mouth, licking and kissing him.

He opened his eyes, seeing a mass of auburn ringlets draped across his stomach. Some of it tumbled down and appeared even brighter against the whiteness of his sheets. She had situated herself with her legs spread across his bed, her feet close to the headboard. He grabbed one of her legs, lifting and pulling her over his body. She pulled herself up on her knees, all the while continuing her assault. She moved past his shaft to lick his balls and he groaned. A moment later, her mouth was wrapped around him again.

Her dark red curls were level with his mouth. He breathed in the scent of her musky arousal and lifted his head, sliding his tongue into her vagina. She hummed her pleasure. The vibrations scorched across his aroused cock. His balls tightened, and he took her clitoris between his teeth. Her muscles contracted and she moaned. The sound of it, the vibrations pulled his orgasm from him. Within moments they lay, relaxed in spent passion.

"Red, if you want to say good morning like that tomorrow, you can."

She chuckled and then shivered. Goose bumps littered her skin, and she pressed against him to warm herself. Keeping an arm anchored around her, he bent down and pulled the sheet over the both of them. He pulled her snugly against his body as she rested her head on his shoulder and buried her face against his neck. Her curls tickled his chin. His muscles relaxed and he sank into his mattress. His mind drifted back to sleep, but a shrill ring brought him awake.

Ren grimaced when he saw the caller ID. He picked up the phone, handed it to Grace, and mouthed the words, "your mother."

She snorted. "Coward." Once again completely oblivious to her nudity, she took the phone. Ren watched in awe as her movements caused her full breasts to sway. Morning light splashed across her skin, adding more honey to her skin tone. She sat with her legs crossed, the sheet unfortunately draped across her lap.

He had never been so wrong about someone based on a first impression. Grace dressed the part of the uptight intellectual snob, but her true sexual personality leaned heavily towards being an exhibitionist.

"Hi, Mama," Grace said. "What's up? Why are you calling from the cell phone."

"Going to play it casual, huh?" her mother said with a chuckle. "Never mind. If I were you, I would've done the same thing. Lord knows I could never control myself around your father."

Heat crept up Grace's neck. She'd never get used to her mother's openness about sex. Well, most of the time it really didn't bother her. But there had been those times when she'd had friends over and, short of blasting the stereo, there was no way you could drown her parents out. She'd always known they had sex. She just didn't want to hear it.

"I wanted you to know we've decided to run back to Austin," Adrienne said.

173

"You're leaving already?" Grace said, trying to control her voice because Ren was tracing a circle with one of his fingers around her nipple. She swatted at his hand, but he ignored her and continued the assault. "But Mama, you just got here."

"Only to check on the house and pick up our mail," Adrienne said. "We should be back on tomorrow or Monday. Your Dad and I decided you were in good hands, no pun intended, so we wanted to check up on things." Her father's voice grumbled in the background. "Bert, it was only a joke. Go stick your head in the sand like you usually do, and pretend like she's still seven years old. She's a grown woman. I'm sure she's had sex before." The blush that had heated Grace's neck and face burned hotter. "Anyhow, Sam was up for a trip, so you don't even have to worry about him."

"You got Sam into the RV?"

Ren abandoned her nipple and she breathed a sigh of relief, until he placed open-mouth kisses on her shoulder. He forged a trail of kisses down her arm and then her hand. Excitement zinged through her as he took her index finger in his mouth, swirling his tongue and sucking on it. He kissed the tip of it and moved on to the next one.

"It was your father's idea. Yes, dear, and I told you it was a good one. Let me tell Grace. We brought one of his sheets and put it in the back of the RV. He's stretched out on it, happy as a clam. Well, anyway, we'll give you a call if we plan to be out of town more than a few days. Don't do anything I wouldn't do." Her father's voice muttered in the background again. "Yes, there are a few things I won't do, Bert."

"They headed out of town with Sam?" Ren asked, as Grace hung up and handed him the phone.

"Yeah, they need to check on things at home. They figured you and Gabriel could keep an eye on me while they were gone."

Okay, so her mother didn't say anything about Gabriel. It was implied, so she really wasn't lying. She jumped up out of the bed and headed for the bathroom.

"What are you doing?"

"I've got work to do, Ren."

She turned on the faucet and splashed water on her face. Knowing she would see smeared mascara, big red hair and ugly stitches, she avoided her reflection in the mirror. A movement caught her eye. Ren stood, his shoulder against the doorjamb, nude and fully aroused. Immediately, her blood shot from warm to hot. She averted her eyes, walked over to the tub, and turned on the water. To hide her nervousness, she plugged up the drain.

"We have to figure out who's doing this to me," she said. "Maybe there's something in that diary that will help. I can't understand is why the Cannons completely obliterated Charlotte from everything. If it hadn't been for this diary, I would have never known about her. Maybe that has something to do with what's been happening."

She turned when he didn't respond. His eyes darkened with desire. Her stomach flip-flopped. Slowly, like a leopard stalking his prey, he walked toward her, his eyes never leaving hers.

"Now, Ren, we have to get to work. We don't have time for that." She held up one of her hands as if to ward him off, but she knew it would do no good. She abandoned the pleading and went right into attack, placing her fisted hands on her hips. "Ren Morello, didn't you get enough last night?" He still didn't say anything, just shook his head. "Well, what do you want?"

"You." His voice was husky with desire, his sensuous lips curving. Heat pooled into her belly. "Wet." He placed his hand on her waist, gently squeezing her skin. Her breath caught in her throat and her heart kicked up another notch.

He leaned forward, removing his left hand to turn off the water. He stepped into the tub and sat down, allowing his hand to slide down her leg and rest just behind her knee. His fingers caressed the vulnerable, soft skin and every objection faded away.

"Grace," he said, sliding his hand around the front of her knee to the inside of her leg. "Come on, honey." His deep resonate voice washed over her, sending a throbbing to the center of her body. "You know you like it wet."

He slid his hand closer to her curls and then lightly brushed his thumb over her clitoris. Any thought of research obliterated with that contact. She gave into him, grabbed a condom he must have brought with him, and stepped into the tub. She smiled, rolled the condom down his length, and sank slowly down onto his shaft.

"You know," she said. "You could tempt a nun."

Chapter Fifteen

Over the next few days, Grace and Ren fell into a schedule of sorts. She would teach her classes, he would pick her up from school, and they would spend the night researching and making love. Well, mostly making love.

Tonight he'd called her a couple of minutes earlier to tell her he would be late. There had been an accident involving two teenager drivers, both claiming the other was at fault, and Ren was stuck cleaning up the mess.

Although they'd argued about it, she headed over to the library. No one else was left in her building, and the library was open until nine at night on Fridays. She could've called her folks, who'd returned the day before, but decided to let it go. Ren would be here soon. This way she could get some research time in.

She gathered her things, locked her door, and headed out of the building. Joe Martin, a graduate teaching assistant, was standing at the end of the hallway, by the front doors.

"Joe, how are you doing today?"

"Fine," he said. "I was supposed to be meeting Dr. Peterson. Have you seen him?"

"No, sorry. I'm the last person left in the building." She walked toward the door. "Is there something I can help you with?"

She turned to face him when he didn't answer. Anger flashed in his eyes, quickly hidden behind his usual affable expression. A slither of fear chilled her. Grace stepped back, wondering if she had mistaken her assumption that she was safe with him.

"No." His voice remained the same usual happy tone. "We were supposed to go over my ideas for my paper for the directed study class I'm taking with him. This is the fourth time he's forgotten. I guess I'll give him a call at home."

He lumbered off in the opposite direction. She took a steadying breath and laughed weakly. To think she'd been frightened by Joe.

She walked out the door and a cold blast of air stung her eyes. Bundling her coat closer, she walked in the direction of the library that sat across the street, between the administration building and the student center. The sun had sunk low in the sky, casting shadows. The campus was almost deserted, being that it was almost six on a Friday night.

She looked both ways down the street, and had started to cross when the screech of tires stopped her in her tracks. A dark car barreled down the street toward her. She froze, forgetting she had the ability to move, not being able to break the connection her eyes had made with the bright headlights. The car was close, but she still didn't run.

A second or two later, her mind finally made the connection, but before she could act, a huge object slammed into her from behind. She flew through the air and landed hard on the sidewalk, her hands bracing her fall. Someone landed on top of her.

Then the body lifted away and she took a painful breath of icy air. She tried to raise herself to her elbows, but a hand rested on her shoulder and she realized someone was saying something to her.

"Dr. Michaels, stay still. You need to take a moment to get your breath back and make sure nothing's broken."

She turned her head and looked up. Joe Martin studied her with worried eyes. She nodded, and he sat back, letting loose a relieved sigh. "Joe..." Her voice came out in a croak. "Thank you."

"You just lay there. Damn, I didn't see the license plate." He looked down the street in the direction of where the car had driven, his eyes narrowed as if he could still see the car and read the plate. His eyes widened and a sigh of what sounded like relief escaped. "Oh, good, here comes your boyfriend. Boy, he looks kind of mad."

Grace opened her eyes again, seeing Ren walking in quick angry strides toward them. Knowing she was in for a lecture, she closed her eyes hoping that would help.

"Grace?" he shouted. In a flurry of steps, he reached her side. "What the hell happened?"

She opened her mouth to tell him, but when she glanced at him, she saw he was directing his question toward Joe. Ren already had his cell phone out and was punching numbers.

"I saw a late model Sedan try to run down Dr. Michaels."

"Grace, can you get up? Nothing's broken?" Ren's had softened his voice, trying to keep from yelling at her again. He helped her sit on the curb, her arms wrapped around her knees, shivering. He took off his jacket and draped it over her shoulders. He put his hands on his hips and looked at her unlikely rescuer.

"Tell me what happened," he said to Joe.

"Well, I decided to do a little research instead of going home. I was about halfway between the history building and the street," Joe said, waving his hand in the direction of the lawn that stretched out in front of the building. "And I saw a dark blue or black, late model Ford bearing down on Dr. Michaels. I dropped my backpack, ran over here, and tackled her." His worried blue eyes turned back to Grace. "I'm really sorry if I hurt you, Dr. Michaels."

"Joe," she said. "You saved my life. Don't be silly. If it weren't for you, I would be in a lot worse shape."

"I never believed what everyone has said about you falling down those stairs," Joe said. "I mean, sure, you do have some accidents, but you would never lie about that." He glanced in Ren's direction, giving him what Ren's Italian grandmother would have called the Evil Eye. "I would think you would have better protection being that the Chief is your beau."

Grace laughed at the old-fashioned term. "He's not my beau," she said, hearing a grunt from Ren. "He's my..."

What the hell was he? They weren't having an affair, and it definitely wasn't a one-night stand anymore.

"He's my friend," she finished.

Ren grunted again in dissatisfaction. Well, what the hell did he expect? The sirens of the ambulance reached her and pain throbbed in her head. She dropped her head to her knees with a groan. Joe had just tackled her and her brains were scrambled. How was she supposed to come up with an explanation about a situation she couldn't explain on a normal day?

Chapter Sixteen

Ren bundled her up and took her back to his house. He drew a bath for her, and let her soak in the tub, relaxing in the warm water with a damp washrag folded over her eyes to help soothe her headache. She heard him talking on the phone from the other room, and about twenty minutes later, she woke from a light, peaceful doze as he rapped lightly on the door.

"Pizza's here. It's the best I could do for tonight."

She nodded. "Sounds wonderful," she said.

He stepped into the bathroom. "Let me help you out of there, honey."

He came forward, holding a towel. "Really, Ren, I'm fine," she protested, but he shook his head. He bent his head. His breath warmed her shoulder just before his lips touched her skin. He kissed a trail to her other shoulder, and placed open mouth kisses down her spine. A wave of heat followed his path, and she shivered.

Ren went down on his knees, bringing himself almost eye level with her rear end. He skimmed his fingers across her flesh and then cupped a round globe in each hand. "You know, Grace, one of the first things I noticed about you was the wonderful ass." He squeezed and caressed each cheek.

"Kind of hard not to notice something that big sticking up in the air." Amusement mixed with desire, deepening her voice.

He playfully swatted her right cheek then rubbed it. "You really don't know your power, lady. I guess that's good, because if you did, I'd surely be dead."

He removed his hands and skimmed one finger down the cleft between her buttocks. She shivered and let out a ragged breath. He eased her legs apart, sliding his finger between her lips. He dipped his finger deeper, wetting it with her juices, and then slid it up to her clitoris bud, massaging it with her own arousal.

He turned her around, and gently pushed her until she rested her back against the wall. She rested her head back against the wall, her eyes closed as he slid two fingers into her. Sparks exploded across her skin as he placed wet kisses down a path from her belly to the apex of her thighs. Delicious heat curled in her belly and shot right down between her thighs. Liquid flowed between her folds as he continued to move his fingers.

He licked her clitoris, then gently teased it with his teeth. She lifted a leg, placing it over his shoulder to give him better access. Her breasts were swollen, her nipples puckered so tight it was almost painful. Before she knew what was happening, Ren pulled away, pushed her leg off of his shoulder and was standing in front of her. She looked at him through half-closed her eyes to see him tugging his zipper down. He pulled both his jeans and his underwear down to mid-thigh.

His long hard shaft sprang free. Grace reached down to grab it. He slapped her hand away.

"No, don't even think about it," he said, his voice rough with desire. "You touch me now, and it'll be over in a second."

Feminine triumph slid through her, because she knew it had been her who had brought him to the edge. Dowdy old college professor that she was, she had aroused him. She heard the crinkle of foil and looked down to find him sheathing himself with a condom. He positioned himself between her legs, nudging them further apart with his muscled thighs.

"Grace, baby, put your hands on my shoulders."

Almost as if she was in a trance, she followed his orders. He slid his hands around to cup her rear end and he lifted her against him. His head fell back, his eyes closed. She wrapped her legs around him, locking her ankles behind his back. She could see his Adam's apple move as he swallowed. He rubbed his long hard length against her mound.

"I'm sorry, baby, I can't wait."

He entered her in one long stroke. She sucked in a breath then released it as he began sliding in and out of her. The muscles beneath her hands bunched and shivered. As he continued his powerful thrusts, her moans grew, encouraging him, begging him to end it, to bring her to orgasm.

"You're so beautiful, Grace," Ren whispered. His voice was harsh with his own arousal. "Christ, you don't even realize..."

He thrust twice more, and all the heat he'd summoned gathered and exploded within her, shattering her into a million pieces.

Her orgasm pulled Ren deeper into her heat, stroking him, milking him. He pulled out once more, and pumped back into her, her name echoing in the bathroom as he shouted his release.

Grace's legs were still wrapped around his waist and his head rested on her shoulder. Her breasts brushed against his chest each time she drew a breath. The only thing he could think of was plunging into her again and losing himself. She was a drug, and he, the willing addict.

He slid his arm around her waist, and placed one hand on the cold tile wall behind her, remembering where they were. Jesus Christ, he had taken her against the wall of his bathroom. He pulled back, and looked down into her face. A sheen of perspiration glossed her skin. A little bead of sweat trickled from the hollow in her throat between her breasts, and she shivered.

Before he could do anything to stop it, a sliver of warmth stole into his chest and curled into his heart. It comforted him, yet at the same time, it scared the hell out of him. He recognized the signs of need and tamped down on them. He refused to let this be about anything but sex.

They were good in bed together. That was it. His passion for her was giving her something she needed. That was all it was about. He drew his hands away from her, letting her feet settle against the bathroom floor again. He stepped back, cutting his eyes away, looking sheepish and uncertain. "So, uh...why don't we heat that pizza up?" he asked.

She wasn't blind. She noticed his change in attitude, demeanor, and he didn't miss the momentary hurt it caused, darting across her face. "Sure," she said, forced cheerfulness in her voice. "I'm starving." She pushed him aside and walked into the bedroom. "You got a shirt I can borrow?"

"Yeah." He pulled one from his dresser, and placed it on the bed. Then, he practically ran out the door. "I'm going to head downstairs and get the pizza warmed up."

He's doing it again, Grace thought, as she finished putting his shirt on and sat down on the bed. He's scared of feeling close to me and he's trying his damnedest to back off.

Maybe she was wrong, but she was sure he knew the difference between making love and sex. She'd never felt so loved, so cherished in her life. He had to be confused by it like she was. If she gave him a little time, he'd figure it out.

With that thought, she headed out the door and down the stairs. She could smell the pizza and heard her stomach rumble. She hoped he figured it out before he pushed her out of his life.

℘CঞR

The next day, Grace sat at her desk at home going over everything that Ren had found for her on the Cannon family. Someone rang her doorbell, and Sam came tearing down the stairs. His claws clicked across the hardwood floor as he raced to the door. She glanced out the front window and saw Julia's little convertible sitting at the curb. By the time she reached the door, Julia was pushing it open.

"Hush, you mongrel," she said with a laugh. She patted his head, and looked up at Grace. "Hey, how's it going?"

"Slow," Grace said. "I was thinking about cleaning out the fridge, if that tells you anything."

"Cleaning out the fridge? Why?"

"All those people brought junk when I fell at school, and I didn't eat half of it. Thank God they brought it in disposable containers. It would take forever to return it all. Come on in and watch me work."

Julia followed Grace into kitchen. "You feeling okay today? You seem sort of tired."

"No, just a little depressed because I'm not getting anywhere with the Cannon family." Julia sat at the table and watched as Grace pull out several containers of casseroles and place them on the counter next to the sink. She started to empty all the food into the sink. "Ren's convinced the reason the mysterious missing sister Charlotte becomes so mysterious and missing is because her husband changed their last name when they moved to Texas. It's just a hunch of his, but I think it's dead on. If there had been some kind of scandal, especially something like suicide or homicide, without the use of computers it would be easy to slip away. It was done all the time back then."

Grace turned on the water and stretched across the counter to turn on the disposal. She flipped the switch and wrinkled her nose. "Good Lord, something smells atrocious!" She took a step back. "It smells absolutely putrid. I let that stuff sit in there too long." Julia jumped out her chair, almost toppling it in the process. "Turn off the water and disposal!" When Grace didn't react, she did it for her.

"Really, Julia, what in the world has gotten into you?" Grace asked, bewildered. Julia seemed frantic, nearly panicked.

"Jules," Gabriel said from the doorway. Neither of the women had heard him come in because of the disposal. "What's the matter?"

"She smelled cyanide in one those casseroles she's throwing away."

"Julia, you silly, I said I smelled something putrid, not cyanide. I don't even know what cyanide smells like."

Gabriel walked over to the sink and looked at the jumble of casseroles. "Do you know which one?"

"Which one smelled like death? No," she said. "They all stunk, Gabriel."

"Can you show me the containers?" he asked.

"They're in the trashcan." She gestured to it. He walked over and pulled out all the containers, smelling each one. "This is the one," he said holding up a medium sized square container. "Do you know who brought this?"

Grace rolled her eyes. "No, there's no way of telling. Why are you two freaking out? Why would there be cyanide in one of the casseroles? I don't smell any poison. I told you, it smelled awful, that's all, like it had gone bad."

Julia tugged on her arm until she turned around to face her. "Grace, cyanide smells like bitter almonds or old gym socks. Does this smell like that to you?" He held it out to Julia, who took a whiff and recoiled, sputtering and nodding. "Grace?" he asked, holding the dish out to her.

Hesitantly, Grace leaned forward and sniffed. The stench akin to a man's locker room assailed her and she drew back, her nose wrinkled. "Ugh!" she said. "It smells like...! Ugh!"

"Old gym socks?" Gabriel finished for her, and she nodded, her eyes widening in sudden fright. "It appears someone brought you a casserole with cyanide in it."

A chill of dread slunk down Grace's spine. "Someone's trying to kill me," she said.

Gabriel was out the door, and striding across the street before Ren had a chance to open the door to his house. Gabriel talked. Ren listened, his face hardening as Gabriel explained what happened. Both men crossed back across the lawn, side-by-side. Ren was on his cell phone.

When they walked through the door, Ren looked at Grace as if to make sure that she was okay. He walked toward her, and stood next to her, looking into the sink.

"Did you eat any of this?" Ren asked, his voice low and controlled.

If he didn't keep a lid on his temper, he was afraid his head would explode. He couldn't believe anyone who knew Grace would want to hurt her. This sweet, sexy funny woman had never done anything to hurt anyone, he was sure of it. But someone had come to her house while she was recovering from her injuries, and brought her something that could have killed her. Not only her, but also someone in her family.

"I can't remember," she said. "Most of the stuff got shoved to the back of the fridge, and I forgot about it. It is almost two weeks old. I should have thrown it out last week, but Mama's been cooking or we've eaten over at your house."

"I need you to tell me who brought you casseroles and which ones you ate. That way, we can eliminate some of the people."

"Well," she said with a sigh. "Ms. Janey brought one that Dad ate all of before I got any. We also ate Mrs. Garvey's chili."

"You had Mrs. Garvey's chili and you didn't tell me?" Gabriel asked.

"You could have had some, but you've been a little busy to think about eating over here," Grace replied with a knowing glance at Julia, who blushed.

"Let me see, Dr. Gump and Dr. Meyers just brought by some tomatoes, and we ate those," Grace continued. "Patsy down the street brought some kind of Jell-O thingy, which we didn't eat. Mrs. Harris brought a green bean casserole we didn't get to. Oh, and Mrs. Peterson brought by a casserole. At least, I'm pretty sure that's what it was. It's hard to tell with Lorna. That's all I can think of, but you better talk to Mom to be sure. I was a little groggy that day."

A siren sounded in the distance, and grew louder by the second. Tires screeched in front of her house, heralding the arrival of one of the deputies.

"I can't seem to get them to understand that they don't need use the siren except in an emergency," Ren said with a sigh.

Gabriel chuckled. "Give them a break, Morello. You're the closest thing they've had to a real detective in this town. And, although I'm going to rip the bastard who is attacking Grace apart, this is the most excitement we've had since that Fowler shooting."

"Jake should have never slept with Gina's sister," Julia said, shaking her head and *tutting*. "If he hadn't, he'd still be in full use of his penis. It's his own damn fault."

Chapter Seventeen

Ren parked in the driveway behind Dawson's BMW and sighed. He really didn't feel like doing this, but he was going to question the jackass. He was almost positive Dawson wasn't behind the attacks, but he definitely had something to do with the break-ins. He hoped the idiot didn't try to fight him on it. If he even thought about challenging him, Ren was sure he would beat the shit out of him.

He climbed the stairs of the porch but before he could reach the top, Dawson barreled out of the house, his arms full of clothes. He skidded to a stop, just inches from running into Ren.

"Morello," he said with a sneer. "What the hell do you want?"

Dawson swallowed twice and his eyes darted from side to side, looking for an escape route.

"Going somewhere?" Ren asked casually. Instead of wrapping his fingers around Dawson's neck, he shoved them into the pockets of his jeans.

"I've decided to head out of town for a few days. Nothing wrong with that."

"Listen, let's cut the bullshit," Ren said. "Where's your girlfriend? I want to see if she has a good casserole recipe I could borrow."

"Ronnie?" Dawson asked. "I have no idea where she is. She said she had to run back to Austin for a few days, and that's the last I've heard from her. She hasn't called and I haven't been able to get a hold of her. She left some items here, but I still have no idea where she is at the moment."

"I thought you and I should have a talk down at the station about some of the things that have been happening with Grace lately," Ren said, clapping a hand firmly against Dawson's shoulder and steering him around. "Why don't you go back into the house, dispose of your things, and then I'll drive us down? It shouldn't take anymore than an hour or two. Then, you can be on your way."

Thirty minutes later, Ren and Darian sat in the Cannon Police Department's one interrogation room, otherwise known as the break room. It was small and square, with an outdated refrigerator, a microwave with a dial timer, and a drink machine that still dispensed glass bottles of soda. There was a corner sink with lime green cabinets, probably installed sometime around 1960. They sat at a long white table that sagged in the middle from years of use. Ren studied the man Grace had thought would make a good husband, trying to figure out what she'd ever saw in the self-absorbed jackass. The man in question was white as sheet and his eyes had the look of a deer about to be hit by a semi-truck.

"Now, you want to tell me what you know about Grace's fall a couple of weeks ago?" he asked, leaning forward with his forearms on the table. "Someone just tried to run her down in their car recently, too. I'd like to hear your thoughts on that, as well."

"I have no idea what you're talking about," Dawson replied. "Grace's fall down the stairs was exactly that—a *fall,* from everything I've heard. She's not the most coordinated woman, in

191

case you haven't realized. And I don't know anything about someone trying to—"

"What I figure," Ren cut in, "is that you've been trying awfully hard to get her out of your way so you can steal her research on the Cannon family." He leaned back in his chair, placed his feet, one crossed over the other, on the table and laced his hands behind his head.

"Research? Why would I have to steal research? I've had several publications, including one book."

"Well, from what I understand, all of your publications are based on your first book. How many times are you going to be able to pass that off without looking like an idiot?" he asked. "Are the head honchos down in Austin giving you grief because you don't publish on a regular basis?"

"What the hell would you know about the publishing world in academia?"

"You must be worried to bring out the big words," Ren said with a mocking smile. "I had a long talk yesterday with Dr. Meyers about getting published. Publish or perish, isn't that the saying?"

Darian didn't say anything.

"See, I know you didn't even do the research for the first book." Ren watched Dawson's eyes widen a little, but he showed no other sign at hearing the news. "Yeah, Grace told me how you stole her research, and then fucked her assistant. Not well done of you."

"You can't prove anything! There is no way you can prove those allegations."

Ren dropped his feet onto the floor, and leaned on the table again. "What's the matter, Dawson? Couldn't find some other cute first-year professor to use? Getting a little old to be hanging out with the research assistants, so where do you get help from now?"

Fear drained from Dawson's eyes, replaced by anger. His pale skin flushed, his whole body went rigid.

"You really are a piece of work, Dawson," Ren said. "What did you do? Get a woman to do the job for you all the way through college?" The anger Ren felt boiled into a full-blown rage. "You're right. I can't prove a thing. It doesn't mean I have to be nice to a user like you."

"Me? A user? You really have some nerve, Morello. What the hell are you?"

Ren shifted in his chair, uncomfortable for the first time.

"Yeah, I know what's going on with you and Grace. Hell, the whole town knows. There isn't much more to talk about around here than who is doing whom. And do you know what they're saying?" When Ren remained silent, he continued. "They're saying it's just a matter of time before you drop her."

"You better be really careful about what you say, Dawson," Ren said, his voice vibrating from the anger.

"What? Did Grace say that she'd let you go? That all she wanted was an affair?" Dawson's lips curved into a thin smile that had nothing to do with humor. "See, I know Grace as well as you do, maybe even better. Did she tell you that she was career-oriented? That she didn't want to get married right now? That's what she told me, too.

"Oh, she'd never think of conniving a way to get you to marry her. That's not our Grace. She's honest to a fault. She was telling the truth about the affair, at the time. But, someday you will tire of her, and what will she have? A broken heart, and an empty house with that mongrel of a dog for company while she watches you screw every bimbo in town."

Ren grabbed Dawson by the front of his shirt and slammed him up against the wall. Satisfaction filled him when Darian's pale skin drained of all color and his eyes bulged almost out of their sockets.

"Listen, Dawson," Ren said from behind clenched teeth. "You're right. I don't have enough on you to arrest you. But I want your sorry ass out of my town anyway. Today. If I ever hear of you coming around Grace again, I'm going to hurt you. You got that? I'll rip your heart out of your chest. Do you understand me?"

Dawson nodded jerkily and swallowed. Ren stepped back and released him with a push that had Dawson stumbling over his own feet, and falling over a chair. Without a word, he jumped up, jerked the door open and ran.

Ren picked up the chair, sat down and took several deep breaths. His heart still slapped against his chest but his anger dissolved quickly into guilt.

He's right. What the hell am I doing with Grace? Sure, he felt attached to her, but that was because they had great sex. He was sure Grace and he would remain friends when they split.

The thought of breaking up knotted his stomach.

He let out an irritated sigh, disgusted with himself. He stood and decided to head home to Grace, trying his best to ignore the trickle of warmth that the thought brought.

℘⊙ℭℜ

Ren knew Grace was waiting for him when he returned from interrogating Darian. He could see through his front window, her sitting in his favorite chair, a glass of wine on the table beside the chair. Uneasiness held him momentarily immobile. He wasn't in the mood to confront any of the accusations that Darian had thrown at him.

He stalked to the living room, and pulled the curtains shut. He plucked Grace out of his chair and sat down, with her straddling his hips. Her husky laugh ignited a fire in his veins, pushing him closer to the edge.

"Well, hello to you, too," she said. She was looked down at him, warmth darkening her eyes. He knew women like Grace confused great sex with love. That was all it was and all it was ever going to be, and neither of them would ever regret it. He would prove to her that this is what they needed.

He caught the back of her neck and jerked her head down, bringing her lips in line with his. Her skin flushed and her eyes dilated, and he knew that she was aroused. He could feel her moist heat even through his jeans. He kissed her, driving his tongue into her mouth, tangling with hers. The hand he had at the nape of her neck slid down her spine. Roughly, he gripped her fleshy hips, forcing her to gyrate to the rhythm he wanted.

He pulled back from the kiss, abruptly, almost violently. He slipped his hands underneath the sweatshirt, his hands repositioning on her bare skin. His fingers flexed almost convulsively as he watched her pull it over her head and throw it on the floor. He realized that not only was she without a bra, she had left her panties off.

Because of their position, her breasts were eye level. He took a nipple into his mouth, pulling it between his teeth. He bit down gently, bringing a ragged moan from her. His hands had drifted up her back and tangled in her hair, gripping it between his fingers. He pulled back and laid his head on the back of the chair, his eyes closed so he could enjoy the sensations.

She slid her hands from his shoulders, down the front of his shirt. Pulling it open, buttons flew and scattered across the floor. Pushing aside the shirt, she placed her hands on his hot skin. Electricity seared through his system as she used the tips of her fingers to trace one nipple then the other. The only thought in his mind was getting inside and feeling her hot wet glove close tightly around him.

"Shit!"

"What?" she asked. Her eyes were barely open.

"Condoms, upstairs. We have to get upstairs."

"No we don't," she said. Her hands were still massaging his chest. She leaned forward, so close her lips brushed his earlobe, her breath in his ear. "Since you have a habit of starting things downstairs, I decided to be prepared for you tonight."

One of her hands left his skin. Then, he heard a crinkle of foil. He opened his eyes. She was holding the condom eye level.

"Grace," he said, his voice ragged with passion. "Now."

He pulled her off of him and stood, struggling out of his shirt. Grace unbuttoned his jeans, slid the zipper down, and was reaching into his briefs when he stilled her hands.

"No, my way." He didn't care if it sounded possessive. He wanted to possess. He wanted to own that beautiful, luscious body, round and so hot and wet for him.

He quickly disposed of his jeans and briefs. He circled Grace, like a leopard stalking his prey, until he stood behind her. He pressed his hardened cock against the cleft between her sweet cheeks. His hands stole around to her belly and he slid one lower until he reached the very core of her heat. While he kept kneading her stomach, one finger glided between her slick folds. He almost came when her sweet juices dampened his finger.

He slid his finger up, brushing it against her swollen clitoris. Guiding her with one hand, he walked her over to the wall.

"Brace your hands against the wall, Grace. That's it, baby. Now, spread your legs."

She followed the instructions and he shifted behind her. He pulled out the condom and threw the wrapper on the floor. He rolled it on, and stepped closer.

"You're going to like it this way. I'm going to be so deep." He placed one hand on her stomach and used his other hand to guide himself into her tight sheath. He stopped before pressing all the way into her. He tightened his hand on her stomach and entered her slowly. Inch by inch, he allowed her heat to surround him.

He wanted to savor her. He wanted her to want him with the same ferocious need that consumed him. She dropped her head forward and her hair fell with it. As he thrust forward, bringing himself in to the hilt, he leaned forward, against her back, and brought his hand to cover her hot, wet sex.

He pushed away her hair with the other hand and began to nibble on her neck. Almost painfully, he kept to the slow rhythm, thrusting in and out with skilled precision. All the while, he continued to whisper crude descriptions of what he was doing to her. He loved the feel of her sweet ass slapping against him as she pushed back, trying to increase the rhythm. He removed his hand, causing her to whimper in protest and placed a hand on each hip to keep the rhythm slow and steady.

He increased the speed slightly, and reached around to caress her clit again. Her moans increased in volume, growing with each thrust. Her inner muscles clamped tight around his cock, pulling him deeper as she began to convulse.

He thrust deeply into her one last time and came. His orgasm swept through him, powerful, tense, every thought in his brain dissolved as he spent himself.

Ren slumped over her, kissing her neck and shoulder, allowing her hair to tickle his face. Her skin was dewy with perspiration, and he breathed in the scent of their spent passion.

"So, how was your day?" she asked with a laugh.

He smiled and kissed her shoulder once more. Life with Grace would always be interesting.

As soon as the thought registered, he stiffened. What the hell was he thinking? This was *not* life with Grace! *This was sex! Great sex!* he thought. It had nothing to do with happily ever after.

He picked up his jeans, put them on, and headed to the kitchen without a word.

Chapter Eighteen

Grace's ears were ringing. It wasn't a continuous ringing. It would ring, then stop, then ring again. She cracked an eye and saw filtered light and realized it was morning. A second after that, Ren yelled out, "Could you get that, Grace?"

Thank God, it was the phone ringing. She kept thinking that she could end up with some kind of permanent damage from all of the injuries. She couldn't have taken ringing in her ears. It would have driven her crazy.

She picked up the phone, without looking at the caller ID.

"Hello," she said.

"Uh, I don't know if I have the wrong number, but I was looking for Ren Morello," a syrupy sweet southern female voice said.

"This is Ren's."

"Well, this is Delta, his ex. Is he anywhere around there?"

A movement caught her eye. Ren stood in the doorway to the bathroom, his chest glistening with water and a towel riding low on his hips. "It's Delta," she whispered and watched all the lusty happiness that had filled his eyes a second before drained, his lips drawing into a thin angry line.

He walked over and took the phone from her. His eyes had turned distant and he gave her his back, heading out of the room. She stood, gingerly testing the sore muscles she'd gotten from their extracurricular activities from the night before. Knowing they had to get some research done, she grabbed the sweats she had worn yesterday and put them on.

After she was dressed, she headed downstairs in search of her shoes. She stopped at the bottom of the stairs, hearing Ren's voice drift out of the kitchen.

"That sounds great, Del, I'm happy for you two." Then there was silence. She turned away, knowing he had deliberately left the bedroom to have the conversation. If he wanted privacy, she would give it to him. Unfortunately, the next string in the conversation stopped her cold.

"No, not seeing anyone seriously." Silence, then. "Oh, that was nobody. Yeah, well, Del, like I said, give my best to Ed and be sure to let my lawyer know. Yeah, sure thing. Bye."

Grief and despair tore at her heart, and ripped it to shreds. She could take the fact he wasn't that serious about her, but to refer to her as *nobody*? That was too much. Before she could stop them, tears welled up and spilled over, coursing down her cheeks.

Ren stopped cold when he reached the doorway and saw Grace standing at the foot of the stairs, crying. Betrayal reared its ugly head. He couldn't believe she'd been eavesdropping. Before he could think he blurted, "Well, you don't have to worry, that was my ex-wife telling me that she's getting married. No need to eavesdrop."

She didn't say anything, just sat on the stairs and put on her tennis shoes. "Just because you answer the phone and you hear a woman's voice, doesn't mean you need to jump to conclusion that I'm running around on you." She still didn't look at him, just rose, and walked around him and into the kitchen. "Grace, you have no right to be mad. I have every right to have a conversation with Delta." She grabbed her purse and walked around him, treating him as if he were invisible.

"You have no right to dictate to me who I can and cannot talk to," he told her.

"I know," she said, her voice just above a whisper. "I would never think I had any rights to you." She wiped away another tear and grabbed her coat off of the banister. "I just don't like being referred to as 'a nobody'."

"That's what you're mad about?" he asked, astonished. "That was nothing."

Grace looked at him. "I can't keep living like this. You don't want anything more. I do. That's the end of it."

Her words sent mind numbing panic racing down Ren's spine. "Grace, honey, we agreed to no strings attached. You said that was fine."

"I know," she said, defeat evident in her tone. Her shoulders were slumped, and he quickly stamped down on the guilt. There was no reason to feel guilty. She'd been the one being nosy. "I know what I agreed to, and I know what you'll give. I'm the one at fault. I fooled myself into thinking this is what I wanted. I was wrong." She looked him in the eye. "But I can't lie to myself anymore. This is over."

"Grace, just let me—" he began.

"No," she said, picking up her coat and draping it over her arm. "You don't need to explain. I understand. You don't want to give anymore. You want nothing holding you down. You know, two years ago—hell, even two weeks ago—I might put up with giving you all the love and understanding. I would've cherished our time together, kept taking all the little things you did to keep yourself separate from me on that level. I would've thought that the pain was worth it."

She gave a humorless laugh. "But you want to know the funny thing? Part of being in love with you has convinced me I'm worth a lot more than you want to give me. The truth is you *are* a coward. You're the nobody because you've decided living in a world with no love is more important than living in a world with pain." She shrugged. "Well, I deserve better than that." She looked directly into his eyes. "I deserve better than you."

She turned and walked out the door, closing it with a quiet click that echoed throughout the foyer. Rage boiled through him. Wasn't that just like a woman? He'd been up front with her. He'd never led her on, letting her think there was something serious between them. He had told her he did not get serious. He'd told her he didn't want the kids and the house. He wanted to be free. He wanted no strings.

He stood staring at the door, wondering why he felt so angry when he'd gotten exactly what he wanted.

Chapter Nineteen

"So when I started to think about it, I thought maybe Lorna Peterson could help you," Dr. Proctor said, pushing up his little horn-rimmed glasses back up his nose. "She was a beauty queen you know, down in south Texas. For good reason—she was just as beautiful then as she is now."

Grace and Dr. Proctor were sitting in his den, drinking hot cocoa and discussing her research. The week had been trying on her nerves and she tried desperately not to let herself grow distracted by thinking about Ren. "I had no idea you and the Petersons were on so close."

"Oh, my yes. Harry and I married a month after I graduated with my doctorate and I was teaching at a small college on the coast. Jason came down one weekend and met her at a bar we went to. One look at Lorna Lang and he was gone."

"Wait a minute," Grace said, surprised. "Lorna Lang? *Lorna's maiden name is Lang?* It was not the same as *Langdon*, but close enough to make the theory Ren had about changing the last name plausible.

"Yes," Dr. Proctor said, settling back in his leather chair. A wistful smile played about his lips and his eyes became dreamy with remembrance. "Lorna and Jason were inseparable that weekend."

"So, where is Lorna actually from?" Grace asked as a shiver of apprehension slid into her stomach.

"Mmm, let me think. I think she was from someplace on the coast, but you know, I may be wrong."

"Do you know anything about her family?"

"No, not much really. I do remember she had a sister who died sometime in the late sixties. There was some talk, at least Jason said there was, that maybe she committed suicide."

Grace sat up straighter. The apprehension twisted into alarm, leaving her cold. "Suicide?"

"Yes. Jason confided in me she'd an aunt who committed suicide, too, and there was some speculation it ran in the family." He took a drink of his hot cocoa, and then continued. "That sort of depression can, you know. I don't think anything was ever proven, but you know how it was if there had been mental disease in your family tree. Back then, they were convinced everyone in the clan would go insane if one person had a problem."

"Yes." Her mind was already working in the direction of what she knew could not be true. Lorna could not be related to the Cannons. That would mean she'd been the one trying to kill her. Grace didn't think Lorna would do something like that. She was a little strange, but Lorna wasn't homicidal. *Was she?*

ℴ)ℛ

The pressure of the case was getting to Ren. Never in his life had a mystery confused him. He knew part of the job was letting go of the ones you couldn't solve. If he didn't, he'd have an ulcer the size of Texas. He leaned his head back, closing his eyes, and pinching the bridge of his nose between his forefinger and thumb.

A sharp knock sounded at his office door, bringing him out of his thoughts. Ms. Janey walked in, gave him the same evil eye she'd been giving him he and Grace had broken up, and slammed some files on his desk.

"You know, Grace broke it off with me," he reminded.

"You must have done something to deserve it." She slammed the door as she left.

Before he had time to call her back in, there was another knock and the door flew open wide. Gabriel stood in the doorway, barely controlled anger simmering in his eyes.

"I was wondering when you were going to make it in," Ren said sarcastically. "Can I help you, Michaels?"

Gabriel raised one eyebrow, and gave him a smile that held no warmth. "Yeah," he said shutting the door behind him. "I've behaved for the last week or so because Dad said to leave you alone, but I want you to know once all this crap is cleared up with Grace, you and I are going to have it out. Oh, and you're lucky Julia loves me, because I convinced her to let me issue the threat. Otherwise, she would have been here last week. There was talk of sharp utensils and your testicles."

Ren snorted. "Well, thank you, Michaels. I won't tell anyone you care for me. It would be embarrassing."

"Smart ass," Gabriel said.

Before Ren could respond, his phone rang. "Hey, Ren, it's J.T." J.T. was an old army buddy of his, who'd gotten out about the same time and became a cop in Corpus Christie.

"Hey, what's up?" Ren said. He flapped his hand and scowled toward his door, doing his best to offer Gabriel unspoken invitation to leave. Gabriel remained where he stood, folding his arms across his chest.

"Well, I did some checking and there was a family with the last name of *Lang* here," J.T. said. "Had a lot of money, old Texas money, if you get my drift." The hairs on the back of Ren's neck stood at attention and a shiver ran down his spine. "Ned Lang was the father, moved here around..." Ren heard a lot of papers shuffling on the other end of the line. "Around 1920, had a few children. One committed suicide while she was locked up in the state hospital." Goosebumps rose on Ren's arms. "He had a son as his only survivor, named Peter, who in turn had two daughters and a son. One of the daughters is dead but the son, Fredrick and daughter, Lorna survived."

"Lorna?" Ren asked, almost afraid to hear the confirmation he knew J. T. would give him.

"Yeah, she was a little bit of a local celebrity down here with Papa's money and the fact that she was a beauty queen."

Beauty queen, Ren thought. His mind raced through a minefield of possibilities. *Jesus Christ.* "Thanks, J.T.," he mumbled.

"No, problem. You think you can make it down here to do some fishing?"

"If I can get this cleared up soon, I might take you up on that offer."

He hung up and looked at Gabriel, who was studying him. "Where's Grace?"

"None of your goddamn—" Gabriel began, but then Ren stood up, his fists balled, his brows narrowed.

"Where is she, Michaels?" he snapped sharply.

"Over at Dr. Proctor's," Gabriel said.

"You take her over?" Ren asked.

"No, she drove herself. It was just down the street so I figured it really didn't matter. What is it? That was something about the case wasn't it?"

Ren shoved him aside as he marched out the door. "Michaels, what the hell are you all letting her run around by herself for? Jesus." As he stormed for the building exit, he called over his shoulder. "Ms. Janey, get me Dr. Arnold Proctor's phone number. Call me when you've got it." He spared her a dark look to quiet any smart remark or argument she might have offered in reply. "The *second* you've got it."

ȘȘ

Grace sat on the edge of the sofa in the Peterson living room and tried not to tap her foot. Every nerve in her body bounced like an out of control Ping-Pong ball. The clank of dishes in the kitchen told Grace Lorna was still making the tea she'd promised. For all Grace knew, she was sharpening her collection of kitchen knives.

I shouldn't have come here, she thought. She knew it, but didn't they say hindsight always saw 20/20? At Dr. Proctor's house, it had seemed like a good idea. Now it just seemed reckless and rather stupid.

Unable to calm herself, she jumped to her feet, nearly capsizing a vase of flowers sitting on the coffee table. She paced nervously in front of the fireplace, trying to think of a reason to call Ren. If she gave Mrs. Peterson a likely excuse, she could probably use some kind of code over the phone to let Ren know that she thought she was in danger.

Embarrassment flooded her. She was starting to sound like Ms. Janey. Talking in code to Ren on the phone, she thought with a chuckle. She realized she was chewing her thumbnail and silently cursed. If she was nervous enough to start a habit that she hadn't succumbed to in years, she was in trouble. Lorna would surely know that something was up if she didn't get her nerves under control. She took a deep breath, and was about to let it out when Lorna burst through the door. It came out as a cough.

"Oh, dear," she said. She set down the tray of tea she had brought with her from the kitchen, and rushed over to pat Grace on the back. "Are you all right?"

Grace looked at Lorna and saw genuine concern filled in her eyes. The fear drained out of her system and she relaxed. There was no way Lorna could fake that. She led Grace by the hand to the couch, and helped her seat herself.

"I brought everything that I could think of—sugar, lemon, creamer and sweetener." She patted Grace on the knee and poured the tea into two dainty ivory cups, trimmed with roses around the tops. She settled into a rocking chair beside the couch. "I do wish more people still took tea. It is amazing how many little things like that have vanished."

"Mmm, I agree," Grace said. "I remember having tea with my Grandma. Every afternoon she served it on this wonderful old service. It had been a wedding gift from her grandmother. She even had a cart she would wheel into the living room."

"So many traditions are being thrown aside," Lorna said, shaking her head. "Young people today have so many misconceptions about what is right from wrong. Take Brandon, my youngest." She paused to take a sip of tea. "He is living with some lawyer up there in New York. Just living with her. No marriage, no ring." She sighed.

"Oh, I didn't know Brandon was serious with anyone." Grace was trying to keep the conversation going so Lorna wouldn't realize she wasn't drinking her tea. There was no way she would take a chance on that. "Maybe they'll get to know each other better and get married."

"You would never live with a man, would you Grace?"

"I already did, Mrs. Peterson. I lived with Darian Dawson. We were engaged, but we did live together, too."

Grace wished she would tell what the woman was thinking. Did she envision Grace as some virginal sacrifice and her plans were now ruined? She decided to be blunt. She couldn't take much more of this idle chitchat.

"So, I came over here because Dr. Proctor thought you might be of some help with my research." Mrs. Peterson gave her a blank look, so she forged ahead before she could wimp out. "I understand that you're from south Texas. Dr. Proctor told me that your maiden name is Lang."

"Yes to both." Lorna sighed heavily and reached over to a potted plant on the end table. She pulled out a gun from within the leaves and pointed it at Grace's chest.

It happened so quickly and unexpectedly that terror like Grace had never known rose up and struck her immobile. Her mind went blank and her mouth refused to work.

"I thought you would take the hint, but you're too stupid to understand what you're doing," Lorna said. "But then, it's unnatural to have a career, dear. Women were not made to work. They should take care of the home. My great-grandmother left her career to be a wife. It is what we were meant to be."

"Your great-grandmother made a career of robbing banks," Grace said in quiet reminder. "She even killed two people."

"Cordelia Cannon was a pillar in this community," Lorna said, her voice rising slightly. Grace watched the barrel of the gun waver as anger made her shake. She took a couple of breaths to calm herself. "She made the perfect mayor's wife.

There was nothing wrong with her. You're not going to sully her memory with this ridiculous research of yours anymore. Not Cordelia, or anyone else in my family."

Sweat gathered at the nape of Grace's neck. A bead of it rolled down her back and she shivered. Stark raving madness shone through Lorna's eyes. *Terrific. Now I notice it,* she thought. She knew she had to do something. No one knew where she was. By the time they figured it out, she was going to be shot and buried somewhere in the loony's yard.

"If you would have just let it be, you would have spared me a lot of trouble," Lorna said, a pleasant smile on her face. "But you wouldn't let it go, and well, I can't let you bring my family name, our hard-earned reputation to ruin, now can I?"

"I won't tell anyone," Grace whispered. "I'll keep everything a secret." Desperation dripped from her voice. Every nerve ending in her body was frozen.

"Grace, Grace, Grace." Lorna shook her head. "Why would I believe a little slut like you? I know what you are and what you do with that Morello character." She shook her head and her lips pouted in apparent disappointment. "You can never trust Italians. They are an insatiable lot. They like to rape and pillage." She stood up and then motioned with her gun. "Now, up you go. I must figure out where to put you so that you won't leave a stain. I'm thinking about the bathroom. If the blood spatters, it will be easier to clean it up."

Grace hesitated, but stood when Mrs. Peterson waved the gun in front of her face to remind her who was in charge. She walked through the doorway that led to a tiled hall. Ivory ceramic tile stretched out before her and Grace knew as soon as they reached the end, she was in trouble. She walked, passing pictures of the Peterson family. It struck her odd that something as normal as wedding pictures or pictures of one of their family vacations were about to witness to something so strange and violent.

The best thing she could do was slow Lorna down. Maybe, just maybe, she could think of something.

"So," she said, trying to think of something to divert her. "Is this a new hobby? Killing people, I mean."

Mrs. Peterson tinkled a little laugh, as if someone had made a witty remark at a cocktail party. "No, of course not. There have been a few others. Why, just recently I took care of that Ronnie character. She was such an easy mark. The little slut. She would have kept that damn Dawson around for weeks. I didn't need someone else to get a hold of your research. All I had to do was run her off the road." Grace's stomach turned and bile rose to her throat. Ren had told her about chasing Darian out of town, and Grace had simply assumed that Ronnie had tagged along with him.

"The most memorable was the winner of the Miss Corpus Christie Pageant," Lorna remarked. "Of course, I didn't have to be as careful about being caught because the technology wasn't what it is today. Poisons were not that easy to detect. She ate some candy, she died and *ta daaaa*."

Grace turned. Lorna struck a pose by putting both of her hands above her head and a pageant smile on her face.

"I was the winner, instead of the runner-up. I should have won anyway."

Knowing this was probably the only chance she would get, Grace pounced. She drove herself into Lorna's midsection, surprising her. Grace encircled the other woman's waist with her arms and pushed her to the ground. Lorna lowered her arms and the gun, squeezing the trigger when she had it level with Grace's shoulder. Heat that stung like a hot poker lanced through her and Grace almost fainted from the pain.

In the next moment, she heard a roar. Lorna looked behind her and shrieked, but still didn't release Grace. Instead, she began to struggle again in earnest. With what little strength she had left, Grace fought back. One shove and both of them were falling, Grace hitting the floor before Lorna. The gun slipped from Lorna's grasp at the impact and, using her good arm, Grace tried to shove Lorna off her. Before she could, Lorna was yanked away and Grace had a startled, bewildered moment to realize Ren had the older woman by the waist. When he set her down, she went at him with her fingernails, shrieking like a banshee about invading her house and unlawful entry.

"Fucking hell!" Ren growled as Lorna caught a piece of his face with one of her nails. The moment allowed for her to dive for the gun, but Ren tackled her. They landed on the floor and Lorna's head slammed into the hard tile. Grace watched Lorna's eyes roll back into her head and she passed out. Ren checked her pulse as Grace tried to pull herself up. The throb in her arm had grown to mind-numbing pain. When he reached her side, he gathered her up close. A wave of nausea made her close her eyes and swallow. She was so cold, and Ren was so warm, so comforting.

"Don't worry, honey. Everything is going to be alright." His lips touched her temple as a swell of agony overwhelmed her. The last thing Grace remembered before the blackness pulled her down was the sound of sirens.

Chapter Twenty

Ren and the Michaels waited over an hour at the hospital while doctors tended to Grace's gunshot wound. Ren stalked the hallways, still recriminating himself for not having protected her. But more than that, he hated himself for what he had done to Grace. She had given him everything he'd asked for, and he'd blamed her for it. He'd let her know that she had meant nothing to him, but that was wrong. She meant everything to him. If he couldn't have her, his life would be unbearable. Pain, bright and strong, lanced through him when he remembered his last words to her.

It was another thirty minutes before Dr. Edwards came out of surgery. He walked down the corridor, looking tired but relieved. "Well, you can rest easy," he said, a weary smile on his face. "She didn't lose that much blood, and she's in stable condition. She's in recovery and should be coming around in a few minutes. I want her to stay in the hospital for at least three days. She'll have to wear a sling to keep the shoulder immobile, but after some rest, should be right as rain."

Ren turned to find a very relieved family unit. Adrienne fell into Bert's arms, crying in relief, while Gabriel folded Julia against him, kissing the top of her head as she clutched him closely. Ren shoved his hands into his pockets and decided to make a quick exit. He thought that he could find out where Grace would be staying and wait for her in the room.

"Ren?" Adrienne asked. "I think that Bert's going to go pick up something for all of us to eat. I figured you would be staying around, too." She waited for his nod and continued. "Well, Bert, get extra for Ren." Bert kissed her on the cheek and left.

"Why don't you have a seat, Ren? You look ready to drop," Julia said.

Too weary to argue, he sunk down in the chair Bert had vacated, and leaned his head on the wall behind him, stretching his legs out in front of him. Adrienne plopped down beside him and he turned his head to find the same radiant smile that Grace had.

"So," she said casually. "When are you going to make nice and give me grandchildren?"

€&#65533;Щ

Ren stepped quietly into Grace's hospital room. The lights had dimmed, but there was a bedside lamp aglow. She appeared to be sleeping as he approached the bed. Her eyes were closed, her hands folded neatly across her bosom. The stark white cotton sheets rose and fell with each breath and the room was heavy with silence. She looked so small on that bed. The smudges beneath her eyes were even more prominent against her pale skin. He'd almost lost her. Even though the doctor had told them she was out of any kind of danger, he couldn't stop the mixture of panic and anger that rose in his throat to choke him.

"What...? Who...?" she said, coming to with a start as he sat down beside her. Her bleary gaze settled upon him. "Oh," she whispered. "Ren."

He thought she might have smiled, but figured it was the drugs. "We need to have a talk, sweetheart, but I'm not sure you're up to it."

"I told you everything I know about Lorna Peterson and the shooting in the ambulance," she said. Any hint of a smile had faded. Her usually lively eyes looked so cold and dead to him. For the first time since deciding it was time to make his move, he was having second thoughts. Panic climbed through him, settling in his stomach. If he couldn't get her to forgive him, he was dead. He wouldn't have a prayer of making her believe in him.

"I know you did," he said. "I'm talking about us, you and me."

She groaned, closing her eyes. "Look, Ren, we settled this, didn't we? I thought you called me a nobody. I told you I didn't like it and wanted a family, and you ran the other direction, squealing like a little girl."

For someone on some serious pain medication, Grace was summoning some fire. "I didn't run squealing like a little girl," Ren said, fighting the urge to grow irritated with her.

"Close enough," she said with a sarcastic snort of laughter as she glanced at him.

"Well, I changed my mind."

"Too late. Thanks for stopping by." She dismissed him by closing her eyes.

"Grace, if I have to haul you out of that bed and spank that delicious ass of yours to get you to pay attention, I'll do it."

Her eyes shot open and then narrowed. "You won't tell me what to do, you big oaf. The only reason you're over here is because you feel guilty that I got shot and you weren't there to protect me. Either that or you're just upset because I figured the whole thing out before you did, and then handled it myself."

"You call this handling it yourself?" he asked, waving a hand to indicate the heavy layers of bandages, the sling on her arm.

"You think you lost, that's all," Grace said. "This way, you get me back, then you dump me so you can win. Well, I can't take it! I can't take the humiliation, so just go away." Her eyes filled with tears.

He felt like the biggest bastard on the face of the earth.

He took her hand. Hers looked so small and delicate in his he couldn't even imagine her fighting off Lorna Peterson. He threaded his fingers through hers and noticed just how cold they were.

"I can't go," he said.

She opened her eyes. Questions and unshed tears filled them.

"See, I have this thing for my landlady," he told her. "I can't walk by those bushes without thinking about her bending over them. I can't look at my stairs without seeing her flying down them." She gave him a watery smile and a small ray of hope invaded his heart.

"I definitely can't cook on that kitchen island without thinking of kissing your breasts or having your legs wrapped tight around me. You invaded my house, babe. I see you in the living room, the bathroom, and I see you especially in bed with me at night. I can't seem to function and staying at work late isn't helping."

Her smile grew then dimmed a little. "How do I know you're not doing this because you're just lonely? You could just want some company and you see me as easy."

"Red, you're funny, sweet, and downright the most sexy, passionate woman I know. But you'll never be easy. I love you, Grace."

"No," she said, her eyes widening in panic. "You don't love me."

She scrambled off of the bed, and he grabbed her hips since he couldn't grab her arm. He kept her from bolting, whether through his strength or her weakness in recovery, he didn't know. He really didn't care. He pushed her gently back down, covering her and anchoring her to the bed. He was careful of her shoulder, but refused to give in.

"You don't want to settle down," she said.

"Why do you say that?" he asked, his voice as soft as a whisper.

She pushed at him and he didn't budge. "My shoulder hurts."

He immediately jumped off of her, and Grace leapt off the bed.

"That was dirty, Grace," he said, wounded. "I didn't take you for a liar."

She inched away from the bed, and he stalked her.

"Liar? My shoulder *is* hurting," she insisted. He jumped on the bed, scrambling over it, trying to reach her on the other side. She lunged to the side and out of his reach.

"I'm not supposed to be out of bed yet," she told him.

"Come back then," he said, with a pointed glance at the mattress.

She backed toward the bathroom, hoping if she locked herself inside, he would leave her alone. He slowly followed her, his breathing a little heavier. She didn't know if winning the pursuit had turned into something more, but a telltale tingle of anticipation inched down her spine.

Before she would succumb to those feelings, she turned and ran into the bathroom. She slammed the door and he heard it lock seconds before he reached out and caught the knob. "Grace, open the door," he said.

"No."

"Honey, talking through the door isn't the way to figure this out," he said. "Come on, please. Let me in."

"No, you hurt me, Ren. I can't go through that again." The pain in her voice sliced through Ren like a knife.

"Okay, I'll lay it on the line." Silence greeted that announcement. He didn't know if he was doing it right, but he had to win. "I can't live without you, baby. I'm not just lonely. I need you, no one else. I wanted you from the first time I saw you, but knew you were a woman who would want to settle down. I tried to stay away from you, but it just wasn't possible."

He leaned his head against the door and reached up to lightly touched the oak with his fingers, willing her to feel the caress on the other side. "I was just too stupid to know that this is what I wanted. I think of you when I open my eyes in the morning and dream about you all night.

"I was wrong. I hurt you. Do me a favor. Marry me and make me pay for it the rest of my life." Silence greeted that statement, and he held his breath. His hope dimmed with each second that passed. Then her steps neared the door. He held his breath as he waited.

The knob rattled, and he stepped back from the door. It opened in a rush, and she stood before him, tears streaming down her face.

"You want to marry me?" she asked.

He nodded. "I want the whole deal. Sam, you, a house full of kids. I want to buy your parents' house, add on ten rooms for all the children I want to have with you. I want your heart, your soul. I want you to be mine in the eyes of God, Texas and the whole damn world. I want you in my bed every night. Hell, I'll fly to Vegas tonight and get married."

She laughed, wiping away the tears from her face. "You can't do that. I know Barney is out of town this weekend. He went to Fort Worth with his brother."

"Grace," he said, his heart almost stuttering to a stop. "Are you saying that you'll marry me?"

"Well, if you think I'm having ten kids, you can forget it." She took a step forward and euphoria swept through him.

"We can compromise on that."

"You have to put up with my family," she said.

"Done. Honey, I'll shave my head and join a cult if it means that I get you."

Grace practically jumped into his arms, her heart beating so fast she thought it would burst through her chest. His arms snaked around her waist, and he lifted her off the ground. He turned and carried her to the bed, stopping beside it. He held her there, her feet a few inches from the ground, determination in his eyes.

"I need an answer, Grace." A strange mix of vulnerability and determination colored his voice.

"Of course I'll marry you, idiot."

He smiled a smile full of love and erotic promises. He moved his hands to her waist, lifted her and placed her on the bed.

"You sure know how to make a guy sweat, woman. I plan on making you pay for that."

He followed her down on the bed, and she said, "I'm counting on that, Chief."

He pulled her into his arms, being careful of her arm. She snuggled against him, his arm anchoring her to his side and her head on his chest, her hand over his heart. The pain in her arm was now down to a twinge thanks to some very wonderful drugs and Ren's soothing body heat. His fingers trailed up and down her spine and she felt her mind drifting into a pleasant numbness.

Several minutes later, he shifted a bit and she looked up at him. Tenderly, he brushed her hair away from her face then brushed his fingers along her jaw. The gentle action belied the frown he wore.

"One last thing," he said, smacking her on her rear end, and, to her way of thinking, liking it too much. "I don't want to return home to find a man on the porch or driveway. That's really getting old."

Her husky laughter filled the room as the last rays of the sun seeped from the sky.

About the Author

Born to an Air Force family at an Army hospital Melissa has always been a little bit screwy. She was further warped by her years of watching *Monty Python* and her strange family. Her love of romance novels developed after accidentally picking up a Linda Howard book. After becoming hooked, she read close to 300 novels in one year, deciding that romance was her true calling instead of the literary short stories and suspenses she had been writing. After many attempts, she realized that romantic comedy, or at least romance with a comic edge was where she was destined to be. Influences in her writing come from Nora Roberts, Jenny Crusie, Susan Andersen, Amanda Quick, Jayne Anne Krentz, Julia Quinn, Christina Dodd, and Lori Foster.

Since her first release in 2004, Melissa has had close to 20 short stories, novellas and novels released with five different publishers (Samhain being her fifth) in a variety of genres and time periods. Those releases include: *The Hired Hand*, a 2005 Eppie Finalist for Contemporary Romance and *Tempting Prudence*, a 2005 CAPA finalist for short erotic romance.

Since she was a military brat, she vowed never to marry military. Alas, fate always has her way with mortals. Her husband is an Air Force major, and together they have their own military brats, two girls, and an adopted dog daughter and they live wherever the military sticks them. Which, she is sure, will always involve heat and bugs only seen on the Animal Discovery Channel. In her spare time, she reads, complains about bugs, travels, cooks, reads some more, watches her DVD collections of *Arrested Development* and *Seinfeld*, and tries to convince her family that she truly is a *delicate genius*. She has yet to achieve her last goal.

She has always believed that romance and humor go hand in hand. Love can conquer all and as Mark Twain said, "Against the assault of laughter, nothing can stand." Combining the two, she hopes she gives her readers a thrilling love story, filled with chuckles along the way, and a happily ever after finish.

To learn more about Melissa, please visit: www.melissaschroeder.net. Send an email to Melissa at Melissa@melissaschroeder.net or join her Yahoo! group to join in the fun with Melissa and her readers: http://groups.yahoo.com/group/Melissaschroederchat and http://groups.yahoo.com/group/Melissaschroedernews

GREAT
CHEAP
FUN

Discover eBooks!

THE FASTEST WAY TO GET THE HOTTEST NAMES

Get your favorite authors on your favorite reader, long before they're
out in print! Ebooks from Samhain go wherever you go, and work with
whatever you carry—Palm, PDF, Mobi, and more.

SAMHAIN
PUBLISHING, LTD

WWW.SAMHAINPUBLISHING.COM